ALSO BY CHRISTIAN KRACHT

Imperium

THE DEAD

THE DEAD

CHRISTIAN KRACHT

TRANSLATED FROM THE GERMAN
BY DANIEL BOWLES

FARRAR, STRAUS AND GIROUX | NEW YORK

Farrar, Straus and Giroux
175 Varick Street, New York 10014

Copyright © 2016 by Verlag Kiepenheuer & Witsch
Translation copyright © 2018 by Daniel Bowles
Printed in the United States of America
Originally published in German in 2016 by Kiepenheuer & Witsch,
Germany, as *Die Toten*
English translation published in the United States by
Farrar, Straus and Giroux
First American edition, 2018

Library of Congress Cataloging-in-Publication Data
Names: Kracht, Christian, 1966– author. | Bowles, Daniel James,
 1981– translator.
Title: The dead : a novel / Christian Kracht ; translated from the
 German by Daniel Bowles.
Other titles: Toten. English
Description: First American edition. | New York : Farrar, Straus
 and Giroux, [2018] | "Originally published in German in 2016 by
 Kiepenheuer & Witsch, Germany, as Die Toten" — ECIP galley.
Identifiers: LCCN 2017051706 | ISBN 9780374139674 (hardcover)
Subjects: LCSH: Motion picture producers and directors—Germany—
 Berlin—Fiction. | Horror films—Production and direction—Fiction.
Classification: LCC PT2671.R225 T6813 2018 | DDC 833/.92—dc23
LC record available at https://lccn.loc.gov/2017051706

Our books may be purchased in bulk for promotional, educational,
or business use. Please contact your local bookseller or the Macmillan
Corporate and Premium Sales Department at 1-800-221-7945, extension
5442, or by e-mail at MacmillanSpecialMarkets@macmillan.com.

www.fsgbooks.com
www.twitter.com/fsgbooks • www.facebook.com/fsgbooks

1   3   5   7   9   10   8   6   4   2

Published with the support of the Swiss Arts Council Pro Helvetia

For Frauke and for Hope

What is life? Thats the question. Something not necessarily leading to a plot.

—VIRGINIA WOOLF

I have only this one heart, no one can know it but me.

—JUN'ICHIRŌ TANIZAKI

PART ONE

序

1.

There hadn't been a rainier May in Tokyo for decades; the smudgy grayness streaking the overcast sky had been dimming to a deep, deep indigo day after day; hardly anyone could recall such cataclysmic quantities of water. Hats, coats, kimonos, uniforms had become shapeless and ill-fitting; book leaves, documents, scrolls, maps began to warp. There, a wayward, imprudent butterfly was struck down in midflight by rainstorms, down to the asphalt, whose water-filled depressions tenaciously reflected the luminous neon signs and paper lamps of restaurants at night: artificial light, cleaved and divided up by the arrhythmic pelting of endless downpours.

A handsome young officer had committed some transgression or other, and he now intended to punish himself in the living room of an altogether nondescript house in the western part of the city.

The lens of the camera was inserted into a corresponding aperture in the wall of the adjoining room, the hole's edges insulated with strips of fabric so that the humming of the apparatus might not disturb the delicate scene within. Kneeling down, the officer opened his white jacket left and right, and with almost imperceptibly trembling yet precisely searching fingertips, he located the correct spot and leaned forward, grasping for the wispy-sharp *tantō* lying before him on a sandalwood block.

He paused, listening, hoping to hear once more the sound of the falling rain, but there was merely a quiet and mechanical whirring behind the wall.

Immediately after the brightly polished tip of the dagger had pierced the bellywrap and the fine white skin of the abdomen underneath, its gentle concavity encircled by only a few black hairs, the blade slid through the soft tissue into the man's innards—and a fountain of gore sprayed sideways toward the exquisite calligraphy of the *kakejiku*.

It looked as if the cherry-red blood had been intentionally spattered by an artist who had shaken out his brush with a single, whiplike motion of his wrist across the scroll hanging there in the alcove in delicate simplicity.

Grunting with pain, the dying man slumped over, nearly losing consciousness, and then with tremendous effort righted himself again. Erect, he drew the knife now lodged in him across his body laterally, from left to right, and then he looked up, past the hole through which the camera was filming him; at length, he spat blood thickened to a glistening gelatinous mass, and his eyes grew dim and vacant. Arrangements had been made to leave the camera running.

After the film had been developed, a copy of it, sealed in oily cellophane, was carried carefully through the rain. The last streetcars ran around eleven o'clock in the evening. One had taken pains to deliver the print punctiliously and on time.

2.

The film director Emil Nägeli, from Bern, sat uncomfortably upright inside the rattletrap metal fuselage of an airplane, biting and tearing at his fingertips. It was spring. How his brow became moist, how he rolled his eyes in nervous tension—believing he could sense the approach of an imminent disaster—how he sucked and gnawed. And while his skin grew sore and red from the pressure of his teeth, he envisioned time and again that the plane would suddenly burst apart in the sky with a flash of light.

It was dreadful; he was at the end of his tether. Polishing his round spectacle lenses, he stood up to visit the lavatory—but raising the toilet lid, to his horror, he was able to see down and out through the hole into the emptiness below, so he returned to his seat in the cabin, drumming the cover page of a glossy magazine with his marred fingertips and eventually asking for a drink that never arrived.

Nägeli was traveling from Zurich to the new Berlin, the spleen of that insecure, unstable nation of Germans. Beneath him the dappled forests of the Thurgau drifted by—for a time the glinting of Lake Constance was visible—and then he espied down below the secluded, desolate villages of a Frankish lowland beset by shadows. The airplane took him ever northward, beyond Dresden, until shapeless clouds once more obscured his view.

Soon they made their tinny, turbulent descent—for some reason he was informed that the plane was to undergo repairs at Berlin's Central Airport; apparently something in the propeller housing was defective. He wiped his clammy forehead with the end of his tie. And then, finally, with apologies, he was served a cup of coffee. Hardly sipping it, he looked out the window into the fathomless white.

His father had died a year ago. All of a sudden, as if his father's passing had perhaps been an initial sign of his own mortality, middle age had set in, unnoticed, overnight, with all its prudishly concealed, secretly suffered mawkishness, its perennial purple self-pity. Now all that would follow was old age, an era of feebleness, and nothing more thereafter but a void that to Nägeli seemed wholly grotesque, which is why he worried at his fingers, the skin of which had now peeled away in milky, translucent little shreds.

At home in Switzerland he had often dreamed of stepping out into his snow-covered garden in winter, stripped naked, of leaning over to perform some breathing exercises and knee bends, and of observing the ravens circling overhead in search of sustenance amid the snow. They glided gracefully beneath leaden skies, without any consciousness of themselves. He would notice neither the numbing cold on his bare feet, nor the crystalline-whirling snowdrifts, nor the tearlet that fell forth into the frost.

Someone would shout *Cut!* and an assistant would prepare a close-up of the tear and approach the actor with a pipette. Nägeli would persist in his squat, holding his pose. At the same time, he would open his eyes widely so he could cry naturally with greater ease should the artificial tear, as was often the case, seem too theatrical.

At that instant Nägeli would become aware of standing both before and behind the camera, and he would feel a malignant, disturbing shudder at this disjointedness, and it was then that he would usually awake.

Emil Nägeli was a rather likeable man; in conversation he would frequently lean forward slightly; he would display great civility that never seemed contrived; blond, soft, yet somewhat stern eyebrows gave way to a pointy Swiss nose; he was sensitive and alert, as if his nerves extended beyond his skin, and consequently was quick to blush; he harbored a healthy skepticism of the entrenched worldviews of others; above his weak chin were set the supple lips of a sulking child; he wore subtly patterned English suits of dark-brown wool whose somewhat abbreviated trouser legs ended in cuffs; he liked to smoke cigarettes, now and then a pipe, and was not a drinker; from watery blue eyes he gazed into a sorrowful and wondrous world.

He pretended to like eating hard-boiled eggs with coarse bread and butter and slices of tomato more than anything else, but in truth he intensely disliked the process of consuming food, which bored and, indeed, occasionally repulsed him. And thus, whenever by supper he had again ingested nothing but coffee, his friends tended to suffer from his unpleasant moods, brought on by his low blood-sugar levels.

Nägeli was losing his light-blond hair, on both his brow as well as his crown; he had begun combing a lengthy strand from his temple over his thus repudiated pate. To conceal the gradual, persistent slackening of his double chin, he had grown a full beard that, disappointed at the result, he had hastily shaven off again; those wrinkly dark-bluish rings under his eyes, which used to appear in the mirror only in the brightness of morning, now no longer faded over the course of the day; his sight, were he to remove his varied spectacles, grew more myopic by degrees, blurry haziness set in; and his full-moon-shaped belly, which stood in marked contrast to the rest of his slender frame, could no longer be sucked in rigorously enough to be made invisible. He began to sense an all-encompassing limpness, an attenuation of the body, a steadily accruing, dumbfounded melancholy in the face of death's impertinence.

3.

Nägeli's father had been a lithe, almost delicate man made somewhat smaller by life; his shirts were always of a certain preciousness, and the very spot at which his trim cuff had enveloped his wrist to reveal both his thin gold wristwatch and his slender hand, tinged with hair only on its side, filled young Emil with a vague, mute, yet almost sexual longing that his own hand might one day rest on the white tablecloth of a sophisticated Bernese restaurant with similar elegance, at once an expression of pantheresque power poised to strike and of genteel restraint.

It was the selfsame hand, his mother had later told him, that had often struck him in the face as a small boy when he had refused to eat his rather lumpy porridge: the very hand, therefore, that had also once flung the punch-bell egg cracker from the breakfast table, together with its egg, against the wall, such that the dismal utensil clattered metallically against the red tiles and the egg then burst, leaving a repellent orange yolk stain on the wall that was still visible, or at least vaguely perceptible there, for years after.

That hand, however, had often protectively reached for Nägeli's own, too, whenever his father and he crossed the streets of Bern and the boy forgot to look left for the automobiles roaring toward them; that hand had then pulled him back onto the sidewalk to safety, it had reassured him, it had warmed him, it had shielded him with the caring touch he so longed for: this same hand he clutched, nearly half a century later, in the hospice room of the Lutheran clinic at Elfenstein, in the capital, and he felt shame at the affectation of this final intimacy.

But where was he supposed to focus his *imawashii* gaze? Up at the ceiling, where everything converged anyway, or straight ahead, over to the deathbed, onto the wooden strip bathed in an icy-green fluorescent light, where commemorative photographs or wishes for recovery might have been pinned?

Or, yes, of course, better to direct it down into the past, to wish soundlessly now, at last, without lament, that those stories would return, the stories he had been told, the ones with the black raven and the black dog, while Emil was rolled up cavernously in his father's silver fox blanket, down at the foot of his parents' bed, groping with his small hand for his father's familiar thumb, for his father's hand.

Philip was what his father had called him his whole life. For forty-five years he flung this cruelty at him, only poorly disguised as humor, as if he didn't know his son's name was Emil; no, as if he did not care to know. Philip, that unyielding, calm, oppressive call—emphasis on the first *i*—and then, whenever the danger of some such punishment, of this or that unpleasant task had been instilled in the child, in the adolescent, then would come the tender, curative call of *Fee-dee-bus*, this belittling familiar form of a name that was not even his.

As his father lay dying, when Nägeli saw him alive for the last time, in Elfenstein, he lifted him gently from the bed, sliding his arms under his back, not knowing whether he was even permitted to do so—but his father was on his deathbed, what authority could forbid him this? The good Doctor Nägeli was now quite as light as a sack of straw, with alarming wrinkles on his back and hindquarters, and covered in dark-blue spots with yellowish edges from being so long abed.

Still, his intimately familiar face, closer and sweeter to Emil than anything else (with its salt-and-pepper beard, which his father had grown on the beach in the summery freshness of Jutland, among the prickly Baltic pines, and then, to the child's disappointment, had abruptly shaved off again, as his son one day would his own; and those two enigmatic blue dots, one on the left side, one on the right, like tattoos, between the ear and the cheek; and that scar, amateurishly sutured, in the little groove between the lower lip and chin), this face now resembled the leathery parchment hide of a hundred-year-old tortoise. The skin had been pulled back from around the ears by the approach of death, and he spoke sotto voce from behind ruinous, putrid, obsidian-colored teeth.

And as the wind blew outside the window in a constant eerie whistle, he asked Emil whether—on the quite obviously blank hospital wall behind him—someone might have noted down Arabic characters, yes, there, look, Philip, my son, and Philip hadn't forgotten to do his military service, had he, and when was he finally going to be discharged from this miserable clinic where his son had had him detained for reasons he could not fathom, and, most important, was he, Philip, ready to perform an insignificant service for a dying old man, a final favor, so to speak, he really couldn't deny him that now, could he?

Shuddering, he waved for Emil to come closer, quite close, so that his father's lips were right against his ear. He chuckled that he had refused to have his teeth cleaned for some time now, and in the last year of his life had consumed nothing but chocolate and warm milk, which was why his oral cavity was festering away and now he needed to whisper something immensely important and definitive to his son.

Tightly squeezing Emil's wrist, he said, yes, come even closer (Nägeli could now smell the old man's musty, mandragoric breath, imagining preposterously that his black teeth were snapping at him as he drew his son closer, quite close, with this very last effort), and then a single, almost powerful *hah* resounded; he was still able to aspirate the sound of the letter *H*, loudly, before a beetle-like rattling issued from the cavern of his father's throat, and he passed away, and Nägeli gently closed his opaque and now streaming eyes.

4.

His elbow propped on a pillow, Masahiko Amakasu lay at home in Tokyo in the large room next to the kitchen, poured himself a few fingers of whiskey, set a record of a Bach sonata on the phonograph, and watched not quite half of the film on his home projector.

He made it no further than the sequence in which the young man, out of whose belly the haft of the knife jutted so lewdly, spouted carnage. Amakasu could not bear to look at blood; such things were deeply repulsive. He felt himself paralyzed by this cinematographically recorded, dehumanized imago of the real.

The whole thing reminded him of a series of sepia-toned photographs from imperial China he had once briefly had in hand, in which one could see an unfortunate fellow being tormented with *lingchi* and sent to his death—the condemned, who during the torture directed his gaze ecstatically heavenward like Saint Sebastian, was being violated with razors; his skin had been flayed, his extremities, finger by finger, sliced off.

Appalled, Amakasu had dropped the pictures as quickly as if they had been coated in contact poison. There were certain things one must neither depict nor duplicate, events in which we became complicit by beholding their representation; that had been enough; no more.

Recently, owing to severely blurred vision, he had sought treatment from a physician friend of his who, after a thorough examination replete with finger-wagging, had diagnosed a fairly serious infection and, while still in the anteroom, plucked out several of his eyelashes with tweezers, causing almost unendurable pain; the problematic lashes had apparently grown inward, toward the eyeball. While he could now focus his eyes very

15

well again, the recollection of that procedure, which couldn't have lasted more than a minute, triggered in him a profound discomfort similar to that produced by the filmic depiction of this suicide.

In recent weeks Amakasu had taken up watching dozens of European feature films: Murnau, Riefenstahl, Renoir, Dreyer. *Die Windmühle* by the Swiss director Emil Nägeli had also been among them, a simple story of an austere Swiss mountain village that recalled in its long-winded narrative style Ozu and Mizoguchi, and for Amakasu represented an attempt to define the transcendental, the spiritual—employing the tools of cinematic art, Nägeli had quite clearly succeeded in illustrating the sacred, the ineffable, within this very uneventfulness.

Occasionally Nägeli's camera lingered long and gratuitously on a coal oven, a log, the braided circlets of hair on the back of a farm girl's head, on her white nape dusted with blonde down, only then to glide fantastically out an open window toward the fir trees and snow-covered mountain heights as if incorporeal, as if the director's camera were a floating spirit.

Amakasu had often dozed off while examining this Swiss film, uncertain whether this was for a few seconds or for whole minutes at a time; his head would flop to the side, and after feeling for a moment that he was flying or perhaps walking underwater, he would awake again with a frightened jolt; the film's suspended, almost abstract mosaics, flickering in hues of gray, had blended with the images from his dreams and covered his consciousness with the violet sheen of an indeterminate fear.

Now, however, he had this repugnant suicide film before him, this documentation of a real and actual death. Shutting off the projector with a curt flick of the hand, Amakasu lit a cigarette, remained sitting in the humid breeze of the table fan, and considered just not sending the reel to Germany, but rather locking it away in the basement archive of the Ministry, leaving it there to be forgotten forever. Gradually, he thought, he was becoming the type of person who has lost all faith, except perhaps faith in the counterfeit.

He abhorred the indomitable secrecy of his country, that reticence that implies everything and says nothing, yet even so, to him, as to every Japanese, foreigners were deeply suspect on account of their soullessness— if, however, one could exploit them and their obtrusive irrelevance to carry out one's unwavering duty to emperor and nation, well, then so be it.

A moth had lost its way in the kitchen and flitted around the refrigerator in circles, its wings beating faintly. Amakasu dried off his plate and glass, returning the dishes carefully to the shelf, and he listened to the steady rap of the rain on the roof of the house.

On second thought, this whole business with the Germans was acceptable after all. Yes, he would send the film to Berlin first thing tomorrow. In the end, it did ultimately boil down to the fact that real sensations coalesce more around a photograph or a film than, say, a verbal utterance or even a slogan. The sufferings of the officer in the film were simultaneously beatific and unbearable, a transfiguration of horror into something loftier, something divine—the Germans would understand this well in their pristine longing for death.

Amakasu walked through the corridor to the bathroom, blew his nose, and twisted a plug from tissue paper to clean out his ears in a bit of Dostoyevskian abandon. He sniffed at it, detecting no scent in those yellow-stained spots, wadded up the paper, and tossed it into the bowl of the modern Western toilet, flushing it and watching as the maelstrom of water, swirling and gurgling indecently, sucked it all down to the final bars of the Bach sonata.

5.

The next morning he rode the streetcar through the rain to the Ministry. Once there, he hung hat and coat behind his office door, ordered tea and some rice, and spent the whole day preparing a letter, in German, to Universum Film AG, which for security reasons that struck even him as a bit exaggerated he did not dictate to his trim (but unfortunately somewhat short-legged) German secretary from the typing pool of the Foreign Ministry, but instead composed himself, on his type-writer, with pale, neatly manicured forefingers that hovered over the keys in two curved arcs.

It was, as Amakasu realized with some satisfaction, a masterwork of manipulation. Self-abasement alter-nated with flattery, reluctant demands with completely untenable promises.

He requested that they please send specialists from Germany, with all haste, who were ready to work in Japan with the excellent lenses of Carl Zeiss and the wholly superior film processing of Agfa, to shoot and produce here, and thereby—if one might phrase it like this—counteract the seeming omnipotence of American cultural imperialism, the manifestations of which had spread like a virus throughout the Shōwa empire, most especially within the realm of film, thus of course making its way onto the street and among the people. This was why, for example, a quota had recently been implemented to protect and foster the beleaguered Japanese film industry.

The catalyst for his decision to approach Germany, that great nation of cinema, he wrote, had been a secret meeting with representatives from the Motion Picture Producers and Distributors of America and a consul general of the United States, during which they had advised Amakasu to reopen the domestic film market (which naturally included the old colonies of Korea and Taiwan as well as Manchukuo, the new overseas territory) to American motion pictures, which were being shut out by introducing said quota, lest they find themselves forced in the future, so sorry to say, to cast not only all villains, but also generally all negatively connoted roles in each and every U.S. production, solely with Japanese-born actors.

Although this, Amakasu wrote, had been a truly elegant chess move that Japan would quite certainly also have chosen to make itself had it been in the American position, their domestic film productions aimed at the Asian market were unfortunately not nearly as influential as those of the United States. We lack, he wrote, the timelessness of plot, the exportability, the universally comprehensible *craftsmanship*; Japanese films were, if one might put it so simply, just not good enough for them to keep pace with the Americans.

And thus arose the compelling notion of allying oneself with Germany, the only country whose cultural foundation deserved as much respect as one's own, hence the wish, hereby stated officially (he bridled at actually putting such nonsense down on paper), to establish a *celluloid axis* between Tokyo and Berlin.

And then came the heart of the matter, the truly important detail amid all the window dressing: they should send him, if he might ask, a German director, or several of them if they liked, but he was thinking primarily of Arnold Fanck, whose *Stürme über dem Mont Blanc* he had watched with deep admiration. Something was conveyed there, behind the things depicted, that had touched his soul; with Fanck behind the camera, one enters a forbidden, mysterious, Hölderlinian zone; this echo chamber is German through and through, but universal as well, which even he as a Japanese can appreciate quite clearly.

He will take the liberty and put it bluntly: If Fanck

21

is not available, might he then hope for Fritz Lang? Friedrich Murnau and Karl Freund are of course already hopelessly and irretrievably in Hollywood, alas, Murnau having even recently died there in an automobile accident.

Oh, the picture *Mädchen in Uniform* also made an extraordinary impression on him and reminded him, if he might be permitted the personal remark, of his own time in boarding schools; to create a film so radical and yet so personal would be of course entirely impossible in this country.

They could also send him Austrian or Dutch directors if they liked. Hotel expenses, travel costs, per diems, lump-sum honoraria—everything would be paid for by the Ministry. That this cultural exchange has the support of the highest echelons is entirely self-evident, and should certain German officials want to visit as well and thereby get to know the Japanese Empire in all its excellence, then they'd be most wholeheartedly welcome.

In closing, he is sending along with the letter a short, modest film to foster a deeper understanding of Japan in the open and honest hope that it might pique the interest of Universum Film AG and thereby the admirable, superior nation of the Germans.

When he had finished the document and signed at the bottom of the very last page with spidery but still elegantly formed ceremonial letters, he replaced the ink ribbon and stashed the used one in his briefcase to burn later, slipping beside it the letter and the film reel he had sealed with wax in a ministerial pouch.

The small package, addressed to the director of UFA himself, was dispatched by diplomatic mail to Berlin that very same day; there, a week later, it was received by the Japanese embassy after largely uneventful flights via Shanghai, Calcutta, and Istanbul and ferried by courier through the well-proportioned avenues of the German capital, though it initially ended up at the film company stuck in an exceedingly managerial pigeonhole clad in elegant mahogany, which was affixed with an under-stated brass placard. Herr Direktor Hugenberg was out of town on vacation, skiing the glaciers of Switzerland.

6.

Nägeli had cried for three days and no more. At night, when sleep eluded him, he read Walser at length and dosed himself with Veronal at around four thirty in the morning. Was it possible he despised his father for having suddenly become so powerless as his life waned, as though the old man had been bitten by the black tarantula of sleep and insensibility? And what had he wanted to say to him at the very end? Had that *H* been the beginning of a word or, perhaps, a sentence? One final thought that might have resolved everything, a sentence if not of pardon, then perhaps at least partly of absolution?

God, there would've been so much to discuss even then, but there was never time for that (at this he kneaded and wrung his hands until they went painfully pink), misunderstandings had piled up (probably also on account of his never publicly voiced insistence to himself that his father had perhaps been inclined toward love between men) that would've taken ten lifetimes to untangle; there you have it, it was a recursive loop, the whole thing, and for that reason he terminated his mourning after three days and dedicated himself wholly to the tasks relating to burial, which he alone, in the Protestant trepidation of his heart, saw himself capable of executing in a humane and proper fashion.

The Swiss Reformed Church duly and conscientiously interred Nägeli senior in the native soil of Bern as Emil had wished. It had been a radiant and sunny winter day, and yet they had had to use pickaxes that morning in order to excavate the frozen earth for the grave.

The Geneva bands of the parson, who with the thoroughly decent iciness of his eulogy took, so to speak, the wind out of the sails of any and all hostile thoughts among the mourners regarding potentially ongoing disagreements, gleamed whiter still than the newly fallen snow of the previous night, which had blanketed memory with a forgiving, powdery layer of oblivion.

The oration had scarcely concluded when someone pulled the cord of a bell, upon whose steadfast tolling the figures dressed in black dispersed like shadows onto the whiteness, to the left and right of the snowbound, refulgently glowing exit.

Nägeli, overtired, wearing sunglasses, mumbled some lines from *The Tempest* that seemed to him appropriate for the occasion, rather than the so very obvious *Hamlet* (and that indirectly described his father, who lay now several fathoms deep and with open eyes at the bottom of the sea), after which he stole away from the open grave, walking backward (was there a slight bow?), when he saw a tall man, unknown to him, broad, lugubrious, red-cheeked, whispering a few words to the parson, saw him try to kiss the hand of the clergyman, who withdrew it resolutely and in haste, disgusted either at this papist familiarity or perhaps at the man's long and dirty fingernails, and with his own outstretched forefinger indignantly pointed the ostensible mourner the way to the cemetery gate.

At a fast clip the man departed; clumsy-footed, limping slightly, and with black jacket skirts aflutter, he hurried down the knoll as if he wanted, as if he just *had* to touch the glacial waters of the Aare River below, for only through the disinfecting properties of the aseptic, cold currents down there in the Matte district might the insincere Lutheran sermon regarding the death of the elder Nägeli be washed away.

The clergyman then invited Emil into the well-heated parsonage for a cup of tea and introduced him there to the new young cantor from Hamburg who contributed a bottle of brandy for their tea, likely also in order to bring the quavering of his hand under control. Eight mahogany chairs were arranged in bourgeois symmetry up against the white wainscoted wall, on which hung a barometer.

The affair with his father was now finally endured and concluded, the German cantor opined, carefully laying two coal briquettes into the woodstove, and Nägeli nodded in affirmation, dwelling no further on which *affair* was meant, nor on who that ominous man out there might have been.

The parson snorted the contents of his nose into a floral handkerchief, tugged searchingly at his white-haired earlobe, and lit a cigarette. No, you're right, one needn't mention the man again, it's over, thank God, it was almost a *Nachtschreck* in broad daylight; cigarette? Nägeli declined with thanks although he would have liked to smoke. A deep drag penetrated the pastor's lungs and reappeared noisily.

At any rate, something incomprehensible had been whispered to the parson, it may have been just a single syllable, a single letter (an *H*, for example? Nägeli shuddered), but they forbade any further thought on the matter and, brandy glasses raised between pointed fingers, hastily toasted one another with Lutheran reserve; there was nothing more to discuss, and even if there were, this was neither the time nor the place for it.

The only subsequent inquiry made concerned Nägeli's fiancée, Ida. Aha, yes, of course, she's in Japan, good grief, that's dreadfully far away, halfway around the globe. Nods of agreement, silence, perhaps some more tea? And the vicar was now already glancing up at the parsonage clock ticking away in Protestant fashion on the wall above the framed psalm verses.

But you know, it's refreshing, it's very nice indeed that Nägeli wants to marry a German woman, the cantor said briskly; the relationship of Switzerland to his, the cantor's, vast homeland up north could be described as reverential, yet at the same time peevishly dismissive, as if the Swiss had taken the enormously profound culture of Germany and, in building on it, had improved it, had made it even more flawless, and now no longer knew how to deal with the coarse, crass original. But didn't his Ida come from an old Baltic, perhaps even Swedish, family?

The parson cast the cantor a needly glare, as if it did not behoove a representative of the Swiss Reformed Church to utter such thoughts aloud, and the circle fell once more into a leaden silence girded by the frosty ticking of the clock.

7.

The parson's sofa, it was the shade of wilting roses, Nägeli noted, storing away this detail so that one day, many years later, long after color film had been invented, he could reproduce it when selecting from the props department of a theater some items of furniture with which he sought to create sets for his final film, as if memory of a hue, of a rare scent, were a spirit that steadily and eternally traveled along at the edge of one's life. At the end of *his* life, Nägeli will say that there had been only five geniuses in a hundred years of cinema: Bresson, Vigo, Dovzhenko, Ozu, and he himself.

Was he right about that? Yes, yes, of course, always. In one sense. Before us we see Dovzhenko's Ukrainian ears of grain, swaying idly and gently in the north wind that sweeps through them in silence; then Jean Vigo's enigmatic, pale wooden barge sailing underneath a shaded bridge; from there, streaming forth, Bresson's bleak, anxious, sacred twilight; and finally we look into Ozu's side-lit rooms, the camera in the Japanese position a good meter lower than is typical in the West, the *shōji* always slid open, but ever present in the frame; in all their endeavors these directors concerned themselves not only with the impossibility of reproducing the color black, but also with depicting the presence of God.

In another sense, Nägeli was of course only just starting to become a great director; he wasn't one yet, or only to some extent. Not long ago, in Paris, he had shot the life and death of Marie Tussaud, a film featuring a scene in which the wax death masks she fashioned of Robespierre, Marie Antoinette, Danton, and Marat were concealed behind a curtain from which they narrated the ghastly events of the French Revolution with the help of intertitles.

That film, however, was censored and mutilated at

the behest of the vile archbishop of Paris, and while Nägeli, bristling, reading Flaubert in German translation at night in the Hotel Meurice (a bulbous glass of mineral water opalized calmly on the night table, over in the armoire a moth flitted from suit to sweater and back), was seized with greater and greater pangs of dejection as he internalized paragraph for paragraph just how bad, how incomplete, how guided by vacuous sloth his own work seemed in comparison, he recalled shortly before falling asleep that his father had invited him to spend a few days with him here in Paris many years before.

He had felt obliged to accept the invitation, despite already then harboring a profound but still unspecified disinclination toward French things in general and Paris in particular, a city that seemed to him worthless, disrespectful, and above all base. Everything was counterfeit with the French, even their commonplaces: *Soyez violent et original dans votre vie, afin d'être réglé et ordinaire comme un bourgeois dans vos œuvres.*

Nägeli was altogether nauseated by the snails in red wine sauce, the frog legs, and the odious rabbit ragout, which his father had extolled to him as, if not delicacies, then the highest expression of a far superior, deeper culture.

Nägeli's father had thus gourmetized himself through

the city while at night in the dingy little guesthouse (for they could only afford such a place), Emil secretly dressed the farmhouse bread he had brought along with shavings of Saanen cheese, with slices of tomato and hard-boiled eggs. For the final evening of their French excursion, Nägeli's father had booked a table at Maxim's months in advance (by letter, while still in Bern, with a pale-violet pencil that only he found eccentric).

Upon entering the sparsely lit, exquisitely furnished restaurant, his father, only with great effort managing to suppress his increasing nervousness, had grandiloquently announced that he had a reservation; yes, indeed, replied the maître d'hôtel, scrutinizing the short foreign man and his decent but modest dark suit with pity, they did have his reservation right here, one moment please, *et voilà, une belle table pour Monsieur Bourgeois et fils?*

No, no, there must be some mistake, his name was Nägeli, Doctor Nägeli, *de Berne*, if you please, and Emil was ashamed of his father's pretentions, and it was only for his sake, after running an endless gauntlet through the dissecting gazes of the other diners and finally arriving at their accorded table beside the door to the fetid men's bathroom, that he bit into the revolting Tournedos Rossini, which were enveloped in grayish bacon, and into the gristly snails (whose rubbery consistency was impervious to chewing, with the result that he swallowed the creatures, almost choking, in a single gulp, as one might a raw oyster), praising the obscenely expensive Bordeaux although he could just as well have drunk fermented grape juice, so little did he understand of wine and so little did it interest him.

A half-inebriated guest had maneuvered himself out of the lavatory, wobbling, wiping his damp hands on the sides of his trousers, and had then squeezed past their table, colliding with it as he turned his hip; and although red wine had sloshed out of their glasses onto the tablecloth, the man had, as the French do, avoided issuing an apology. The stench of ammonia wafted around Emil, beneath which hung, furtively heavy and sweet, the bouquet of excrement.

8.

These ceaseless thoughts of his dead father had clouded his mind in Paris. Dejectedly he left the city, marred for him once more by reading Flaubert, for Scandinavia. After the Madame Tussaud debacle he was to produce his first sound film for the Danish Nordisk studio, but Nägeli didn't manage to shoot a single meter of film, and instead began to exorcise the whole disaster in his mind by way of ceaseless movement through space: by traveling around aimlessly.

All the while, not the slightest idea occurred to him; he bristled in his thoughts at the notion that the squawking of actors would henceforth interfere with the much more profound language of the visual, that the floating, lyrical motion of the camera would now be subject to the acoustic clumsiness of mediocre dialogue.

He spent a few weeks in Gotland, went for walks on the beach, met an old, prematurely aged friend, collected leaves, then journeyed up through the pallid rains of Sørlandet to meet Hamsun.

Nägeli had planned, on behalf of Nordisk, to discuss with the unapproachable, recalcitrant Norwegian a possible film adaptation of his novel *Mysteries*—Hamsun kept Nägeli waiting for hours on a wooden bench in front of his home, only apple slices and water set out, while upstairs in the house the Poet indulged in yogic contortions.

In those days Nägeli was hedged in by a constant, extended, gray sense of suspension; finally, his secretary sent him UFA's invitation, formulated with Teutonic precision, to travel to Berlin, an invitation that reached him at the post office in Oslo. Hamsun, meanwhile, remained disinterested and dismissive. Nägeli took the train south again, toward Gothenburg, then to Malmö, and the weather remained bleak.

Having finally dozed off in the railroad car, he saw in a dream his father's wrinkly neck, the dots of his medical tattoos, the pallor of his kind face covered in age spots, his silvered hair spilling down a nape furrowed like the crevices in a wasteland, his intensely pale-blue, slightly oblique Kyrgyz eyes, and finally, much later, the death mask on the wall of the hospital room, over in the alcove, and the shadows of the Swiss birch trees sweeping gently over it.

9.

Masahiko Amakasu's childhood, in his receding memory as dull and lackluster as a winter's sky, had been that of a precocious, peculiar boy who at not yet three years of age read the newspaper aloud to his parents, a boy who gushed theatrically—he had now barely turned five—about precisely elaborated, sublimely nuanced suicidal fantasies, and in his parents' garden at night secretly excavated pits underneath the gorse bushes to hide his considerable collection of violent picture books, the possession of which had been forbidden him under threat of severe beatings.

Masahiko was sent off to boarding school early, too early, of course; he had not reckoned with the fact that his parents, who had always seemed so liberal, modern, and educated, would commit him to one of the Empire's most merciless flogging parlors—though whether this had occurred out of ignorance or Mr. and Mrs. Amakasu were trying in some way to build his character he was never able to find out.

Their seeming open-mindedness was on shallow ground, however; his own grandmother had adhered so much to the old traditions that she had had her teeth lacquered black—even then already a vanished ideal of beauty.

Every year during the autumn holidays they would travel by railroad northeast to Hokkaidō to gather mushrooms and marvel at the glorious transformation of the foliage, the affirming, melancholy-tinged serenity to which both his father and his mother had looked forward all summer long.

No sooner had the family set up its picnic area (his mother carefully spreading out a snow-colored linen sheet and bedecking it with tankards, black-and-red lacquered boxes, and bottles of almond milk and beer, while above them the leaves of maple trees, larches, and beeches shimmered in a hundred thousand ecstatic shades of color) than young Masahiko liked to disappear behind some tree, allegedly to play, in order to picture to himself there in great detail, after successfully liberating his hiding place from insects fumbling about, the spectacle of his own funeral.

In it his mother, quite openly wailing, would sit before his urn, as would his father, reproaching himself extravagantly in soft silence while gnawing off the insides of his cheeks, and even his classmates, those who had hung him up, the undersized and almost pathologically quiet Masahiko, on a coat hook by the elastic band of his underwear every morning for several weeks before their geography lesson, even they would stand there mute in their navy-blue school uniforms, somewhat off to the side, intimidated by the nearness of death, while the sun raged intermittently through the leaves above.

One of his teachers would step forward, slender, infirm, and bespectacled, and would rub his temple with the inside of his wrist, asserting that he had only ever had the best of intentions, but now he was forced to admit how misguided, indeed, how disastrously damaging his cruel regimen had been (as had, for example, his use of a fishing rod as an instrument of chastisement).

Illuminating this fiction in his mind had filled the boy with such blissful shudders that he tore his pants down and began to rub his lower body against the tree bark in ever more vigorous motions, and when he then imagined his parents culling his skeletal remains from the ashes with chopsticks, a meager and unfortunately all too brief spray of sparks shot off behind his eyes, somewhere in his brain's nucleus accumbens, and the boy ejaculated, fluidlessly and softly panting, on the linden tree.

His knees shaky, he staggered back to his oblivious parents (his mother usually awoke from her afternoon nap at this moment), who now invited him to take part in their beloved family ritual: lying in the autumn leaves, their mushroom baskets beside them, and reading aloud from the poems of Heinrich Heine, which his father, an emeritus professor of German at Tohoku University, had strained to translate into Japanese and now, under the influence of two or three savored beers that lubricated his voice, was declaiming heavenward in the original German, not without humor switching the *R* with the *L* in his delivery. Oh, how Masahiko *hated* his father!

Masahiko had of course taught himself the German language long ago, and now he inwardly squirmed and writhed at the merely half-feigned speech impediments of his father, who, while inevitably proud of his son's genius, at the same time felt an extraordinary unease about it; Masahiko seemed intensely creepy to him, much as the deep sea and the blindly groping *leviathan* reputed to lurk down there in its eternal dark might terrify anyone.

His son, who at not quite nine years of age had mastered seven languages, *and* who was in the process of teaching himself Sanskrit, who, smiling shyly, would write down complex algorithms while masticating his breakfast rice, would compose brooding concerti on their piano at home, and would read Heine in German, seemed to his father possessed by a merciless demon forcing the child into an ever more grotesque thirst for knowledge. Some parents might wish for such a talented child, whereas Masahiko only filled the Amakasus with horror.

Sometimes they would sit together before a small carton on the floor and gaze at photographs of him as an infant, of his first attempts at walking, of his delighted splashing in the wooden tub or grasping a colorful rubber ball, and then they would feel a thoroughly crushing sadness, as if they were seeking to conjure up in those images that frozen, irretrievable time solely through the power of their longing, as if they sensed their child were being snatched from them most unnaturally.

Related to the feelings of the Ainu, those ancient inhabitants of Japan who sometimes refused to be photographed because they feared that fixing their likeness would rob them of their soul, Masahiko's parents occasionally felt, conversely, that these likenesses were their true son, and that the boy growing up there beside them was merely a replica, an unreal mirror version, a dread homunculus.

10.

When had his sexuality begun to take wing out of the baser regions of those childish fantasies of repression and death, rising to actual carnality? Early, early indeed; he must have been nine or ten years old, Masahiko.

There had been a governess, whose slender, clean forearms, covered in vulpine down, protruded from her violet-checked little dress when she, her tunic hiked up high, had thrown her much-too-skinny stork legs over his as they lay prone together, cheek to cheek, leafing through a picture album that depicted the victory of the Japanese army over the cowardly retreating Soviets in Chinese Mukden. The girl's breath had smelled of biscuits.

And while he had felt the weight of her legs and the contractions of her muscles, as well as the hopeful, high trembling of the respiratory system connected to them, he had inserted his forefinger into her half-open, moist oral cavity. She, in turn, had called his name softly and whispered: *iku!*

Thereafter, they had lain together in a tight embrace and listened to the wind, which scratched a twig on the *shōji*. He had loved her more than he would ever love anyone. Four months later, she died in a rather insignificant automobile accident in Tokyo; the steering column of the vehicle, which she should not have been driving in the first place on account of her youth, had squeezed her against the seat and collapsed her lung; glass rained kaleidoscopically, and blood gushed from her mouth like jelly.

11.

His father had really hit him only once, this was in the face with the back side of his clenched fist; Masahiko bit his fingernails, bit them until there was nothing worthwhile there left to bite, and so the boy soon assaulted his toenails, too. One afternoon, his mother led him to his father's studio, saying she no longer knew what to do, just look at his toenails, they're almost entirely gone, completely gnawed off—and the boy had timidly curled his toes toward the floor to hide them as if they were retractable claws, only to receive in the next instant that wholly unexpected wallop, the blunt, drastic vehemence of which sent him hurtling backward and tumbling to the unpolished wooden floor like an unthreaded marionette.

His greater loathing was reserved for his mother, however, because she had delivered him to his fate and then not defended him; while falling he had been able to make out in her face something akin to consenting amazement, her expression contracting in the middle of her furrowed brow—though one might have also read it as astonishment at the severity of both the punishment and the abrupt appearance of his father's aggression—but as if the pent-up rage at Masahiko's disconcerting thirst for knowledge had found its natural expression in that backhand, it was clear that she had also secretly welcomed the strike and even endorsed it.

The boy lay whimpering on the ground, the ringing thunderous sound of a bell in his ears; Mr. Amakasu rubbed his throbbing hand. On his desk the small, round pale-violet paper snippets that the paternal hole puncher had spewed out for years to the child's delight and that, as an infant, he had always placed in his mouth to taste sank imperceptibly deeper into the indentations on the writing surface as if ashamed. The tropical bird over in the aviary, which they had bought as an expression of their unbourgeoisness, had nibbled with disinterest on a cookie.

12.

Whether it was Doctor Nägeli himself or perhaps his
wife who had decided to give little Emil a rabbit can no
longer really be pieced together. In any case, propped
up there in the shed one day outside the windows of
the yellow-carpeted playroom was a splendid wooden
cage in which the animal sat, face and paws expec-
tantly, almost slyly, directed ahead, staring at Emil,
and Emil stared back, spellbound, and gave him the
name Sebastian.

Emil had known from children's books what rabbits
liked to eat—if he approached the animal, however, to
feed it a carrot, he was bitten fiercely on the fingertip;
the child was utterly startled, having been shielded until
then in the thought that existence and the world were,
in their very essence, civilized. Never before had he experienced the indecent and indiscriminate savagery of
nature.

Sebastian had been an intractable white albino with

red eyes, and little Emil had loved him with an ardency edged with pain. Thus, without ever being able to approach the animal, the boy cleaned out its cage every couple of days, stuck the tips of his fingers through the wire mesh of the little stall door, was bitten again and again, for hours raptly contemplating the twitching whiskers on the dear pink nose that turned warily toward him, and observed as the soft paws slid food about.

Emil longed to be able to stroke Sebastian's silky fur, to embrace and pet the animal, bringing him bushels of dandelion leaves he had picked in the meadows, yet there was no opportunity for rapprochement, only the perhaps naïve thought that if he treated the rabbit lovingly it would one day love him in turn.

The rabbit stall emitted the deplorable and sharp reek of the animal's acridly pungent feces. The little dark-green pressed food pellets that his mother would bring home in brown paper bags and that he would stick in his mouth to sample tasted vaguely like rubber.

Sebastian ate them anyway; delicate, fresh dandelion or mass-produced feed, it was all the same to the rabbit. Once the neighbor's cat crept into his parents' garden, and Emil opened the stall door so that his Sebastian would have someone to play with. The rabbit, however, chased after the intruder across the lawn, hissing murderous snarls, its fur puffed up on end, and the cat vanished in panicked fear.

That small, pointed, nerbling rabbit mouth was now appearing to the boy every night in his dreams; but when he tried to wake up, he would tumble out of bed and then lie there on the floor in the hopeless darkness of the nursery, crying for help, incapable of distinguishing up from down and left from right; this confusion was so primordial that even his mother—after running from her bedroom two floors up on account of her child's shrieks, seizing and shaking the wailing Emil, turning on the lights, and imparting to him words of reassurance and comfort—was incapable of allaying her hollering son's inexorable, screaming disorientation for quite some time.

He felt as if his mother weren't able to reach him, as if he were floating underwater, shackled forever in the half sleep of that nightmare, and his mother were standing on the other side of a membrane that imprisoned him, calling and caressing him from without, but that there was no way for him ever to reach the other side.

How childish that had been. Luminous day had hardly materialized, the room's green-plaid curtains had scarcely been torn open, and the familiar garden and the attendant shadows of the firs tremulously projected by that curative camera obscura onto his childhood wallpaper—where the pleasingly repeated arrays of branches and cherry blossoms validated the soothing panorama of his innocent horizon of experience—when the fears faded away, warded off by the genial light of morning. The witches under his bed withdrew and did not dare emerge again during the day.

Lying recumbent on his parents' silken sofa that afternoon, Emil had stuffed a pillow under his neck and lost himself for hours in the cloud formations developing in the sky outside the window, had drifted off to sleep, waking up seconds later, six hours later, and in this intermediate world he learned of his special gift to curse someone just one single time in life and to have this curse come true one hundred percent.

While lying there, he had also spotted a very special tree a decent distance away that he would see time and again during his life; he discovered it not only in Switzerland, but also on the Baltic coast of Germany, in Italian Somaliland, in Japan, and in Siberia, and only much later, in the latter third of his life, did he realize, this time while astride a toilet, that this would be the tree he would see at the moment of his death, not in benightedness like his father, but clearly and happily, and in full consciousness.

When he returned home early one day from a school field trip the children had taken to the caves of Saint

Beatus on Lake Thun—according to legend a place where the eremitic monk had driven a red dragon down into the water with ceaseless, shouted prayers—he found Sebastian's cage empty.

Weeping, Emil ran through the yard, calling for his rabbit, scouring the house first, then the little street that intersected a busier one at the curve, and when he began to make leaflets with a hastily but nonetheless carefully drawn rabbit on them to distribute throughout the neighborhood, his mother appeared and told him in a quiet voice that Doctor Nägeli had seized the rabbit by its ears and given it to the neighbors, a crude farming family, who that same day had killed the animal and flayed the white fur from it, and what's the matter? The rabbit had only ever bitten him anyway, he hadn't been able to play with him or feed him, it was better this way, and Emil really oughtn't look so crestfallen.

Nägeli was seated on the train. The memory of Sebastian into which he had fallen had not even lasted a second. He shot up—while, outside, a nondescript vernal landscape drew past—and suddenly he again heard his mother telling him via telephone (the connection oddly cushioning her voice) that his great-aunt was still locked outside and she was coughing so loudly and no one could endure the noise. In winter and summer alike they had forced his aunt to sleep in the barn—presumably it was whooping cough or tuberculosis—and at some point this aunt had of course slashed her throat with a straight razor because she was so lonely.

But how can anyone possibly live with something like that, he had asked his mother over the telephone, and he was told that's just how it was. Sometimes his throat seemed to close up when he reflected upon the remorselessness and brutality of his family.

13.

Many months later, after he had already been in Japan for some time, and following an exhilarating but also thoroughly exhausting hike that led him first past green-budding rice terraces, then over desolate, darkly desaturated hills, Nägeli came upon a wooden hut at the end of a gently ascending path that nature seemed to have reclaimed. The structure's situation in the landscape elicited in him a profound sense of absolute harmony and proportion.

Pine forests yielded to placidly jagged ridges, the half-concealed foothills of which trailed off into infinitude, into a haziness caused by ground fog, as if they had been cut from translucent colored paper. The hut, which now lay at some distance before and slightly below him, seemed so very fragile, its earthen foundation having been erected in an almost makeshift fashion.

He had approached the dwelling cautiously and tapped hesitantly on the door with his fingernail. The Japanese, he was later told, would not have done this because only foxes, those ominous manifestations of treachery, would tap softly with their tail when they desired entry—a human being would have clapped his hands.

The peasants therefore peered out through a small hidden peephole before inviting the stranger in, and Nägeli slid the *fusuma* aside and bowed, and his spectacles almost fell off. Before them sat clay bowls of rice, tea, pickled cucumbers, onions, radishes—they were too poor for meat; how glorious the simplicity of these people seemed, who lived and worked in solitude, far from all modern comforts like electric light, flush toilets, and other such things.

Although with a really only quite limited command of the language (ten, perhaps fifteen, words accented with Swiss gutturals), Nägeli had admired and turned the teacups with gentle gestures amid the muted candlelight, as if he, a blond *gaijin*, were capable of deciphering

centuries of their distinguished culture in the craftsmanship of these vessels, and when a smiling old man
then poured him some tea, he held the cup carefully and
reverently in both hands, bowing toward him. How
touchingly different from the vulgar people of his homeland, he thought. The Japanese were imbued with being,
with the presentness of the universe.

And while he drank tea and the mood in the room
grew ever more reflective, he recalled all at once having often been sent as a boy into the mountains by his
father to the peasant families in Bernese Romandy, to
Rougemont, Château-d'Œx, and to Gruyère, up to the
late-summery pastures and mountain meadows, in
order to help with the harvest—they were the same
peasants whom his father had once wheedled out of
centuries-old carved and colorfully painted timber
beams, which he then resold at the antiquities dealers in
Bern for fifty times the cost.

These country folk had been coarse and ugly, the
palms of their hands riddled with little cuts and other
vestiges of their decades of field work; in their dark,
dusty parlors it had smelled of warm beer, boiled ham,
and raw milk; they let their goats sleep with them in
their bedrooms; their dialect sounded bovine and earthy.

The little boy had been afraid of their forthright,
beastly manner of slapping each other on the shoulder

and drinking themselves stupid and thereby sinking into a frequently hours-long, sullen reticence. He sensed that they also mistrusted him, but the pact between them and his father regarding the timber beams, which had appeared so mysterious to the child, probably had to be fulfilled, even if the peasants found the boy rather burdensome and if he in turn was repelled by them.

At night he would pull over his face the tattered checked bedspread that so stank of rancid ham in the fervent hope that they would not seek him out. In one of the most vivid longings of his childhood, he would often dig holes for himself, to excavate murky pits in whose crude gloom he might hide himself from the world.

Now, however, in the sparse intimacy of this Japanese farmhouse, he felt these people's unassuming simplicity to be like a magic shroud in which one could conceal oneself protectively. Without uttering a word they made up a plain mattress for him and insinuated with gestures that he ought to go to sleep now, since eerie creatures roamed about the hut in the forest, spirits and witches, hirsute and bug-eyed. He mustn't listen to any noises at night, and above all and under no circumstances, please, was he to whistle in the dark.

Reluctantly and halfheartedly, however, after hovering for a while between sleep and our world (and when the urge to void his bladder grew too strong), he ventured forth to find the latrine in the darkness. After groping his way on warm floorboards down a short corridor that was only navigable on account of the peasants' noisy breathing, he took his seat on the wooden box, listening to the raindrops gently dripping from the leaves outside in front of the *shōji*. He suppressed the desire to whistle, though in doing so a single inadvertent note may have escaped his pursed lips.

In the morning, fortified a little by an unsatisfying breakfast, which consisted of several rice cakes and a little sake, he hiked back down into the bright, sunlit lowland over which clouds drifted like carefree afterthoughts.

14.

Masahiko Amakasu's boarding school was purported to be one of the best in the country: ivy-entwined, dark-red brick buildings that weren't especially impressive skirted a woodland; there was a small, murky lake or pond where from March onward colorfully painted wooden model boats were sent floating in sporting competition like reveries; and off at some distance a pretty hill rose gently and enticingly, the scaling of which numbered among the first pursuits of the newcomers.

Masahiko shared his dormitory room with seven other boys, who, on the very evening of his arrival, seized him and held him down while two lads laughingly emptied his plaid suitcase, holding it up open and letting its contents spill to the ground: the German books, the linen napkins his mother had packed for him, the sheets of music, the microscope, the chopstick set fashioned from yew wood, the bar of chocolate, the small bronze Buddha, and the teddy bear, which they immediately pounced on, tearing off its arms and legs with lavish cruelty, as well as the button eyes his mother had attached with needle and thread.

Masahiko didn't scream or cry, only grew more and more unresponsive and taciturn, and no longer spoke unless he was called on by a teacher in class or had to read something aloud; he had no friends, although he made note of the ringleader of the boys who had destroyed his stuffed animal so as to lure him by some ploy, many months later when the bully had long forgotten the incident, into the woods adjoining the school.

There, after having gone missing for twelve whole hours and just as the school was on the verge of calling the police, the boy in question was spotted again, bound to a tree, physically unharmed, but unhinged and incapable of speaking about what had befallen him or who had tied him up.

That boy suffered wretched nightmares afterward, screaming in his sleep at such unbearable volume that the teachers had to look in on him dozens of times during the night; after several days he was granted leave from the school, was later taken out of the boarding school entirely, and spent the next years of his life in a sanatorium for children near Osaka, in a soundproofed isolation room painted pale green.

The punishments the school meted out to the boys for the slightest infractions could hardly be surpassed in their inventiveness and tedium. Woken up at half past three in the morning, the boys had to carry a precisely specified number of bricks up and down a hillside, two stones each for the least offense, four and more, for example, if a button on a uniform jacket had not been closed according to regulations, or if the fingertips of their white gloves were stained, or if one had encountered a more senior pupil on the gravel path and had not doffed one's cap quickly enough, and so forth. Up to twelve bricks could be accumulated in this way, after which point one was moved to the next worst level of punishment; if they had to answer for thirteen or more bricks, therefore, the boys were whipped with an elastically whizzing fishing rod into the palm of their open hand, which had first been coated in salt.

Never did it cross anyone's mind, incidentally, that it could have been quiet Masahiko who had maltreated the bully, so he was not punished—but there were, nevertheless, suspicions wafting about in the boarding school air, so heavy with rumors and untruths, and the other children and even the teaching staff began to avoid Masahiko as though he were incurably ill, as though he trailed around with him an abhorrent shadow.

15.

Only the German teacher, Mr. Kikuchi—who was no longer at all certain whether he was still employed by the German intelligence service, since the reports on the moods and mental states of his countrymen that he had drafted for years and passed along to the German legation in Tokyo were neither acknowledged nor remarked upon—found an approach to young Masahiko and in so doing recognized him as a phenomenal genius.

Kikuchi had, as a young man, been something of a dancer, ballet, before the First World War, in Vienna, in Michel Fokine's ensemble. Now, back in his home country, long tempered by his liberating, manly, athletic experiences in central Europe, he taught Japan's spoiled young elite who, in his eyes, tended toward mediocrity and were pathologically conformist.

But as these things go, his letters were by no means ignored, but read intently, and by Wilhelm Solf himself at that, the then-ambassador of the German Empire in Japan. And when those reports began making more frequent mention of a highly intelligent boy who both spoke and read German perfectly and who, obviously feeling at ease with German culture, had even cheerfully mastered Sanskrit in his insatiable thirst for knowledge, Solf the Indologist sent word (and this was the very first response from the Germans Mr. Kikuchi ever received) that one ought to look after this young butterfly, please, lavish upon him encouragement and friendship; sometimes the benevolent ministrations of a single adult were sufficient to help a child such as this blossom. Naturally, Kikuchi wished to do nothing less.

On his free day, Ambassador Solf had himself chauffeured to a park near the boarding school so that, from a bench, he might secretly observe young Masahiko on one of his excursions into the city that Kikuchi-sensei supervised. As the sunbeams cast splotches of light across the park lawn, Solf, to maintain appearances, fed the contents of a rolled-up paper sack of flaxseeds to a scurry of squirrels, who first timidly, then ever more assertively, attended to the kernels dropped so heedlessly under the bench as the ambassador's roaming eyes, concealed behind sunglasses, assayed the boy from a safe distance. On the surface, Masahiko admittedly evinced negligible differences to other Japanese adolescents but all the same let something of his extraordinary character shine through in the exuberant game of badminton against his teacher Kikuchi, something that deeply impressed the diplomat.

Solf chose to ignore the fact that Kikuchi-sensei, diving after the shuttlecock, was quite obviously in love, noting down instead the precision of the ensnarement Masahiko employed to keep the white-haired man so animatedly engaged. The elastic choreography was a masterwork of manipulation; if the teacher exercised a bit of restraint, then the boy grazed his opponent with his arm when returning the shuttlecock; if moves were made to attack, then he dropped to his back, pulling the panting Kikuchi down with him into the silky bed of grass.

The game of *wakashūdō*, the old tradition of the

beautiful young man, the *bishōnen*, who is submissive to his teacher, was staged perfectly, and observing it gave Solf a pleasant shudder and the certainty that this very boy was the one to sponsor and instrumentalize, to gradually cultivate into a man who decades later, even after his, Solf's, death, would prove to be extraordinarily useful.

And thus it happened that Masahiko Amakasu began to work for the German Reich without ever knowing it. Kikuchi himself was arrested for unknown reasons and released again a short time later—the boy had already left the school for a military academy—given an allowance, and dismissed from school service.

Masahiko, meanwhile, was henceforth to remain in Solf's shadow theater: the clandestine transfer of a certain payment here; there the promotion of his father to a better position at the university; and here, then—you're welcome—the opening of a new, modern hair salon in the capital under his mother's management . . . yes, Masahiko remained ignorant of everything.

Even after he graduated with full honors and distinctions from the academy, when he was urged to begin a promising career at the Ministry—provided, of course, he passed the entrance examination—no one besides Solf knew of the young man's involvement with the German Reich. And, to no one's astonishment, he bested his class on four successive tests, which assessed not Masahiko's astonishing intelligence, but solely his disposition toward and undying loyalty to the emperor, descendant of the sun goddess Amaterasu.

The seed had thus been planted, and nothing was to stifle his future growth, his meteoric rise: not Masahiko's ostensible disdain for the Western world, nor the German predilection for conquest and the debasement of other peoples, an inclination the young man was able to comprehend with such emotional precision that it seemed he had somehow spliced his own soul into the German one with ethereal wires.

16.

And Kikuchi-sensei? He gave him forth, his boy, into the world. After scarcely a year (his arrest was ignored) he was sent into retirement, and an abyss of free time opened itself before him, an endless ocean of idleness.

He was alarmed, then turned inward and realized with gentle satisfaction that he did in fact still have a few things to attend to. First of all he wanted to have the unattractive steel teeth removed that had once been screwed into his jaw—he had too often partaken of sweets when he was a child.

Motivated by the fear of anticipated torture that was eating away at him and to tame his body and his mind, he began visiting the sport club late every afternoon to learn the art of archery.

They respected him there, and he showed skill and athletic elegance, and whenever he raised the bow over his brow and emptied his being, allowing it to become one with arrow and target, he succeeded in causing not only Masahiko's countenance to vanish, but also the incessant monstrous thoughts of his teeth and their impending surgical excision.

After launching a pair of arrows, he would slide like a spirit in white socks into the back room, following the painstaking rules of *kyūdō*, and bow to the red solar circle of the flag on the wall above him, before fetching the next two arrows lying ready for him there on a table.

And whenever he would make his way home late in the evening, riding the streetcar through lively neighborhoods, he had archery to thank that he no longer felt the loneliness of age, which had wrapped itself around him like a flayed rabbit pelt since his retirement. He knew he would always be able to make himself tea at home, eat some rice, and observe the shadows.

Hesitantly, almost timidly, in order not to disturb the delicate idea, he began to ponder the possibility of adopting another hobby. One day, he imagined with a smile, he would collect porcelain thimbles. And the steel teeth? He left them in his mouth. He never heard from the Germans, from Ambassador Solf, again. One final time a small sum of money arrived, which he saved to treat himself, on his last birthday before his death, to a wonderful dinner in an upscale restaurant in the capital.

17.

Long after Kikuchi-sensei had become ashes, young Masahiko one day traveled out to the cliffs of Tōjinbō. A late snow had fallen, driven down from the north. It was achingly cold. The railroad journey ended in Sakai, where the snowbound citadel of Maruoka shrouded itself in an impenetrable wintry fog. Swaddled in scarf and coat, Masahiko had clapped his gloves together to warm himself and boarded an unheated autobus at the train station square out to the crags; he was the sole passenger.

Having recently turned thirty, he had taken up the habit of smoking and lit himself a cigarette. The autobus had departed for the city again, swathed in a turbid puff of diesel fumes. He held the little yellow flame of the match up to his face as the sea now stretched out before him, ashen and hazy and calm. Doubtless no oak leaves lay at his feet.

He saw the basalt cliffs extending left and right, the towering scab of a long-dried wound carved into the earth millennia ago. In the lull of late afternoon, a young girl stood teetering at the precipice and, after a few seconds of uncertainty and hesitation, plunged over the cliffs, a falling shadow.

Masahiko stamped out his cigarette and ran stumbling to the spot where the woman had only just been standing. He looked over the edge at the rutted, unmistakably sharp umber rocks below, and when, despite shielding his eyes as a sailor would, he could make out no one and nothing but a purple-and-red handkerchief, he carefully clambered down backward for a half hour until, now at the bottom, he nearly slipped on a spongy, faintly crackling bed of kelp. It was slowly getting dark. He had reached the seashore below.

He lit one match after another, cupping his gloved fingers protectively around the flame. A flashlight would be helpful right about now. Damn, the matchbox was empty. He called out a couple of times: no answer, nothing, only the gentle, clear scouring of the lonely, cold sea. He searched the shore and the embankment; something had moved back there. It was only a dark-gray seagull pecking for food in the algal salad.

On a wet rock, he discovered some oxidized, dark-brown blood; here was where she might have landed, hit her head, here—removing the glove, he gently touched the spot with the tip of his finger; impossible to say whether the patch was fresh or had been there for years. In complete darkness now, the moonless sky could no longer be distinguished from the sea.

He hurried a couple of hundred paces along the coast to the west, his hands half-raised before him, until stopping at a grotto from which soft light shone, either a flickering candle or an oil lamp. Cautiously, he stepped onto the yellow-lit patch of shore and approached the entrance.

Cowering inside was a young woman, her back leaned against the cave wall. She waved him over. Her hair was disheveled and shaggy, and aside from a scrap of leather covering her torso she was naked, and she had painted her legs and arms and face crimson.

This couldn't be the same woman who had just been standing on the rocks above. She seized him, throwing him to the ground, and sat astride Masahiko's shoulders. He squirmed and tossed back and forth; he could feel her solid, sinewy thighs, she was extraordinarily muscular, and he was unable to escape her. From her crotch poured forth a repellent stench of rot and pestilence.

It was now as if rifts in time were opening up; blackish-gray clouds appeared on the horizon; maize sprouted in the most improbable places; vines slithered up around a colossal statue of the stone Buddha; winged animals drawn by a child—half mouse, half dragon— were scurrying around on their heads, upside down; everywhere it reeked of ammonia; a tall, dark tree of a man whose face was obscured by shadows whispered a few times: *Hah*.

He dug and pressed into her flanks with his fingers, pounded on her with his fists, but it was no use. Like a repugnant succubus she held him captive, but then she abruptly released him, wailing, took him in her arms, stroked his face, and caressed him, now cooing a flutter of incomprehensible, soft words of comfort and succor.

She was an aristocrat, yes, she blurted out after

crouching once more against the cavern wall, and she was being held here against her will. It was so very wretched, and her hardship was great; she was truly sorry, she had only been trying to keep him here, she hadn't seen another human being in months.

Finally she began softly to weep and lamented that she was subsisting on kelp and rainwater, and sometimes, when the hunger was no longer endurable, she would catch and kill a seagull and drink its warm blood.

Masahiko saw the bones of dozens of birds and innumerable fish lying scattered around the damp mud floor of the cave, in the dark corners small stones had been piled up carefully into temple shapes, and he saw that she had tried in vain to build a fire with wet driftwood.

And the woman who had plunged off the cliffs before, that wasn't her? No, of course not, she hadn't left the shore in months, there was no escape from this place, the cliff face was much too steep to ascend. At first she'd tried every morning to walk along the beach in search of help and nourishment, but after a while there was nothing else but a dense, horrendous fog—not a soul, nothing, it was the end of the world.

Along with the tattered shift, these three candles here, those couple of matches were all she still possessed;

after they were gone, the dreadful darkness would hold sway in her cave. But how had she come to this place, who had cast her ashore? She could no longer remember anything, she said, one day after she'd been locked out of her chambers in Maruoka, she'd fallen asleep before her door in the hallway of the citadel and awoken here on this snow-sown beach, her body and visage colored with red paint.

They had to get out of here, Masahiko said, he'd help her escape, and he thrust a half bar of chocolate into her dirty hand, but she replied, no, there was no point, it was her fate to remain here forever at the edge of the earth to eat raw seagulls and worms, and the night sky would be her coffin, and the moon her grave lantern.

Masahiko then held her in his arms and whispered that he was going to get help now, she ought to be patient for just a short while longer, and he draped his coat over her shoulders and carefully fed her the chocolate. Please don't go, she cried in a tremulous lament, and he answered softly, she shouldn't give up, there was always hope, it was because of her that he had come to this bleak shore, and he would soon return with a doctor, with blankets, and with rice.

And while she continued to weep and implore, he left the cave and strode onto the beach, then hurried back to the place where he had seen the bloodstain on the rock, and while the sobbing could only barely be heard in the distance, he climbed up the slope, painstakingly groping his way, until after a good hour of ascent he had reached the edge of the bluff, pulling himself up onto flat ground, which now seemed to him a stable, safe place, sheltered from the terrible dreamworld down below.

It had begun to snow again, and he marched back through a freshly white crystalline world in the approximate direction of Sakai or wherever he supposed the city to be, and with every step that distanced him from the cliffs, he forgot the events in the cave and forgot about the crying, lonely, ruined woman in it whom he had promised a quick return.

Only several months later, at home in Tokyo, did she appear to him again, standing by his bed, in the fearful moments just before awakening; or every so often, in the furtive gloom of a movie theater, whenever a film had not yet begun: then he would see her before him, her red-painted face turned away from him, cowering off beneath the movie screen, beside the ruffled velvet curtain.

18.

When we see someone suffering, we can find it within ourselves to pardon him for just about anything. Back in Zurich from Scandinavia, Nägeli had driven out past the city gates to Oerlikon to be shown a film at the local office of Danish Nordisk that, in a way, might be counted among the beginnings of his craft: August Blom's *Vampyrdanserinden* of 1912—a clumsy though not incapably staged dramalet that began to burn right in the middle of the show, as the film had obviously been loaded incorrectly.

The screening was discontinued; stepping out of the booth, the projectionist issued multiple apologies after having fiddled about with a fire extinguisher to spray foam that now bashfully dribbled down the inside of the little projection booth window.

Nägeli remained riveted in his seat, his soul touched by the kaleidoscope of hypnotic magenta, of green, of blue, of yellow, indeed, of turquoise, created on the screen before him by the light beam from the still blithely projecting apparatus that shot through the firefighting foam, and he wondered (his head cocked slightly) whether the future invention of color film wouldn't have much more sweeping aesthetic consequences than now nascent sound film. Two things were fundamentally opposed to one another, no?—color and film; it was evident, though, that a depiction of reality with an instrument as metaphysical as the film camera (that crucial but disembodied organ) would always have to be in black-and-white. Color—that psychotic *lūдus*, that crude chaos of the retina—indeed, it was pointless to show it.

All of a sudden Ida came to mind—sublime, refined Ida—and he saw before him her freckled skin, her fair-haired curls that, pertly peeking forth from under a dark-blue beret, often framed the just-finished picture over which she had been leaning, lost in her drawing. Ida!

How precious those holidays on the Baltic coast of Germany had been: they had already danced a quickstep at breakfast in that white hotel, she had eaten a piece of torte sumptuously dolloped with whipped cream, then came the walk down to a sea lined with dressing cabins cheerfully striped in blue and white, where wave after wave poured, tidelessly, tamely, onto the shore.

And so they had gone into the water for a refreshing dip when quite suddenly the emerald whirl of a wave struck him, pulling him under, and he resurfaced, faltering and huffing and happy in the iridescent summer light; his hand raised in reassuring greeting, he had seen her standing there on the beach, deeply tanned in her navy-blue bathing suit, the tips of her delicate toes half-buried in the sand, her slim hands wrenched before her gaping mouth out of worry for him; then, when she saw Nägeli standing safe and sound, she had smiled in relief; there were roses, sprays of seawater, the homey, nutlike scent of seaweed, the shrieks of children, the pale-pink foam from seashells, the barking of dogs, the bones of coral, a cloudless, ecstatic sky, her slender upper arms, pearls instead of eyes; not for a single moment more did he think of his dying father, mumbling to himself instead as he stood in the ocean up to his loins: This is exactly how my childhood smelled.

And in his mind colored subject and colored object became one, the beholder and the beheld, as if for a few seconds he had been permitted to break through that veil of time that keeps us mortals from apprehending the cosmology of our existence.

Then later, up in the hotel room at the very end of a long corridor carpeted in coconut runners, Nägeli, aroused by a strong desire induced mainly by the effect of the hot sun, had torn from Ida's body (the summery skin of her nape already smelled indecently of pistachios in the elevator, of damp oat straw) her still-wet bathing suit and mounted her from behind, huffing and puffing, on the double bed, as if she were a mare in heat—in the course of which it seemed to him as though Ida, turned away from him toward the wall, were nonetheless stifling a soundless yawn.

Nägeli remained seated there in the projection room for a long time while the screen above shone white and blank and inconsequential, as if both it and he had lost their meaning. The soapy foam had all slid off. He began to pack himself a pipe, paying no heed to the tobacco crumbs that fluttered onto his shoes, nor to the warm little tear under his eye.

So now his father was gone. His shade was forever rent from time. He felt as if now, finally, the myriad possibilities of his imagination were embracing him; he snuggled deep down into his suit coat and dozed off, the pipe cupped in his hand on the armrest.

And then, snoring imperceptibly (sleep is a rose, as the Russians say), he was watching a matte-gray, completely plotless film that lasted for hours, and in this dream he saw an oddly quaint Europe, aquiver by morning; he saw crooked façades of half-timbered houses, which appeared to be perpetually crammed against each other, pushing and shoving; poets in pointed caps, living inside under twisted roofs, composing their dithyrambs in springtime, before dawn; magnificently resonant church bells, heralding Eichendorffian mysteries, calling burghers to early Mass with their peals; he heard the imperturbable *clop-clop-clop* of horse hooves; he saw splendidly heaping silver platters of cheeses, ham, blood sausage, and grapes, whose cloying, meaty aromas wafted over the cobblestone marketplaces, and saw the breakfast beers as well, hastily sloshing their way to the tables, tankard by tankard; he saw hanging above him massive, black, wrought-iron lamps, unlit by day, dangling down now like empty cages (those in which people were displayed as punishment in former times); and he saw the room at the clinic after his father's body had been taken away, and the deathbed, and the pillow with an indentation in the middle that looked as though it had been arranged precisely so as to ensure that the impression of the back of his father's head would only remain eloquent and visible for a short time and then cease to exist.

19.

At the very end, on the last day of his final year at school, Masahiko had obtained the key to the attic from Kikuchi-sensei's locker and surreptitiously entered the top floor of the boarding school. He had barred the metal door behind him, crawled under the roof braces to the place where the insulating wood shavings protruded out a good bit from the roof ridge, and seated himself on a crossbeam, where he ate two rice balls.

The resinous aroma of the wood and the familiar taste of his snack filled him with a great, deep satisfaction, permitting him some distance from his actual scheme: to destroy this school that had humiliated and debased him for years. Dangling his feet, he watched a rat scurry along the inner edge of the roof and vanish into its lair amid the shadowy planks. Then he sat there motionless for quite some time.

Next, he reached into the trouser pocket of his uniform and produced the matchbox, turning it absentmindedly around and around and finally laying it down neatly on the crossbeam beside him, sprang onto the attic floor in one leap, left that place again by the little door and hung the key back on the hook in Kikuchi's school locker unnoticed, then strolled into the schoolyard to squat down and attend to a somewhat tricky mathematical problem that concerned, among other things, the proof of existence of several polynomial rings.

And while he sat there thus, making his calculations, the earthy smoke of the fire reached his nose even before he could see it. He immersed himself in his notes, the school bell was rung, and then, piercingly, a dissonant siren sounded. Pupils rushed out of the main entrance like startled crows, gathered in the courtyard, and gawked up, mesmerized, at the crest of the building from which the tongues of yellow-red flames darted, accompanied by thick black smoke, growing ever taller and blazing in joyful arousal up into the sky.

Although the fire brigade was on the scene not a half hour later with two fire engines and a considerable squad of brave uniformed men, the school could not be saved. A tremendous column of billowing smoke rose aloft, and the flames consumed everything, spreading to the gymnasium and obliterating the classrooms, the dormitories, the dining hall, and the teachers' offices with their own special furious greed.

Thousands of files and composition books fueled the flames, hundreds of rubber erasers melted away in a sizzle, pencils and paintbrushes vaporized steadily, even that unspeakable pile of bricks of which the pupils had had to avail themselves in the early morning became a black beacon, streaked with soot.

Masahiko crept away, scaled the hill near the boarding school, sat down in the grass, and watched the fire from a distance, as if he were looking through a microscope or rather a telescope held to the eye the wrong way around.

While tiny grasshoppers sprang beside him out of the weeds, the instructions from the teachers and the fire brigade, shouted through a megaphone, reached his ears curiously muffled. He lay down on his back and observed an incipient little cloud that joined up in the pale-blue sky with a larger one. We live not only in a world of thoughts, he reflected, but also in a world of things. And the past? It was always more interesting than the present.

PART TWO

破

20.

Some weeks after he had dispatched the film and letter to Germany, Amakasu, squeezed into his tuxedo, had been chauffeured early one evening to the American legation for a reception, where the world-famous actor Charles Chaplin, then on a reconnoitering tour of Japan with his manservant, Toraichi Kono, was to be honored.

Those droll films in which Chaplin played a down-and-out fellow plagued by bouts of bad luck who still managed to prevail against all odds were enjoying fantastic success in Japan. Something about the inner, utterly anarchic expression of that short, shabbily dressed, always melancholically amused, mustachioed hero, something in his lived sangfroid, stirred the Japanese soul deeply; they applauded his cinematographic escapades, and his revolt against authority, usually embodied by cretinous policemen, was felt by the audience to be extremely liberating.

Amakasu had caught himself several times in one or the other cinema in Ginza slapping himself on the thigh or laughing freely and without inhibition. It was indeed quite extraordinary what took place up there on-screen; the blows of fate that little prole suffered and then his inevitable victories were at once unsettling and exhilarating.

Now then: Amakasu ascended the four or five stone steps from the gravel path to the main entrance of the embassy, illuminated by floodlights ablaze, a bowing servant took his sodden homburg and umbrella, and a white-gloved officer hastened to salute him, Amakasu nodding as he passed.

In the resplendently lit reception halls things were festive—a local jazz band made sincere attempts to play entertaining but not too obtrusive standards; the swell of dozens of voices reached his ears. Over there was the Dutch ambassador (pederast), there a prominent Chinese Communist (compulsive gambler), smoking in the corner with pointy fingers an Italian colonel (impotent). Amakasu caught sight of the geriatric prime minister, Inukai, bowed toward him to an appropriate depth, his hands flat against the seam of his trousers, and then, smiling, reached into a silver dish presented to him in order to affix one of the pretty pins to his lapel—small, crossed Japanese and American flags.

That was him in the back, my goodness, there was

Chaplin, svelte and trim, the curly hair on his temples tinged with silver, absolutely charming and, yes, very rakish in his black tuxedo, a glass of Champagne in his left hand, in his right a cigar, encircled by three attractive, giggling Japanese women and a jovially muttering bearded admiral, standing next to a tower of orchids that was artfully arranged, to be sure, but with American immoderateness.

Chaplin laughed quite openly at a joke and then quickly covered his mouth with both hands as though he were ashamed of the condition of his teeth, and a black lock of hair fell to his brow, quivering. He looked nothing at all like he did in his films, Amakasu thought; he more resembled a small, likeable rodent, perhaps even a fox.

A Japanese man came sauntering by and handed Amakasu a clinking glass of whiskey—it was Toraichi Kono, Chaplin's smirking assistant, who was already so stone drunk that he morphed back from American to Japanese only as he approached, and this looked labored and unnatural. Of course, he said, of course he knew who Amakasu was, charmed, really. He smelled quite faintly of something old, something unwashed.

Chaplin himself now came stumbling up; Amakasu was unable to say whether his lurching was put on or genuine, but Chaplin had already seized both his hands and was pumping them up and down and relating immediately and outright that he had just seen *Tokyo Chorus* by Ozu yesterday, and it was a fantastic *masterpiece*, and he was now firmly resolved to keep making silent films, like Ozu. He, Chaplin, was first and foremost a mime, and he could say without false modesty that in this capacity he was a singular master.

In this country it was said of cinemas that they were *gardens of electric shadows*, wasn't that a truly wonderful description now that, unfortunately, *Sous les toits de Paris* was being whistled everywhere? (René Clair's sound film was showing quite successfully in Tokyo movie theaters at that time.) And Amakasu noticed how extraordinarily charismatic and intelligent Chaplin seemed after all, and how dangerous this enemy would be, and how much power his culture was capable of exerting, and above all how closely related camera and machine gun were.

He recalled the film reel with the gruesome flick he had sent to Berlin several weeks earlier, and a fleeting doubt stirred in him about whether he had done entirely the right thing—maybe it would have been better had he mailed a more wholesome film, something pleasant, something funny, shots of the *shōshimin* perhaps, inconsequential tales of the trials and tribulations of the lower classes, and he bit himself quickly and inconspicuously on the lower lip, and Chaplin, who harbored an exceptionally sensitive awareness of those around him, gently took the arm of the Japanese man and suggested they leave this quite excessively extravagant reception (for he, too, knew who the unobtrusive Amakasu was) and dine together at the Imperial Hotel, among friends of the cinema, and Amakasu, whose diplomatic skill had abandoned him for one careless second, consented, relieved, feeling simultaneous honor and shame.

21.

And so they drove in a convoy, sitting behind windshield wiper blades that swept away the rain in hypnotizing semicircles, through the dazzling, glittering Ginza district to the Imperial Hotel, a peculiar, eccentric box built by the American architect Frank Lloyd Wright that had always reminded Amakasu of vinechoked Hindu or Maya temples, of the parody of a venerable Babylonian shrine, with its hanging gardens and labyrinthine rivulets, water baths, walls of flowers, and ponds.

For reasons unknown to him, however, he had never ventured inside, and so entering the reception hall, its temperature regulated by immense, invisible machines, proved an unexpected, welcome surprise—the aseptic cool dispelled the stifling stickiness of the natural climate just outside, the rain-damp suit and the dress shirt underneath suddenly became pleasantly clammy layers on his skin, causing him to shiver softly and envision quartz crystals, stacked up by the tens of thousands, bewildering and fathomless in their frigid mathematics.

Farther inside the hotel then, Amakasu hit his head twice, how vexing this was; jagged corners protruded into the lobby unexpectedly, the walls were porous and pockmarked like solidified lava rock, and sconces encased in concrete gave off a matte yellow, pointing the way through the dimly lit corridors, until the group, now a dozen people, was led into the elegant private room of a dining hall where they were served cold Kiku-Masamune wine and vanishingly small crispy fish glazed in sea salt. They took their seats, and at once Amakasu was forced to think of freshly fallen snow, and one of the guests loaded a Goldberg hand camera and cheerily filmed those gathered.

A young German woman had joined them at the *shimoza*, the least important seat at the table. Tasting the little fish, she grimaced, then absentmindedly sucked on a lemon wedge. Amakasu liked her freckles, he found them quaint, and her fashionable aviator uniform fetching, and he slid a pretty clay dish with pickled radish toward her. She smiled and lit a cigarette. Amakasu returned her smile with a graciousness of which he had not thought himself capable.

Chaplin's driver, Kono (Amakasu had already demoted him in his mind), meanwhile, clapped his hands, holding forth, wooden sake cup upraised, cigarette holder between his teeth. Japanese culture, he said, borrowed and perfected phenomena just as sugar was refined; everything here was essentially of Chinese provenance, but China was a country whose slovenliness was no longer acceptable, for the China we knew today was largely shaped by the vulgar bric-a-brac of the Manchus, these ridiculous, petty-minded trinkets of the Qing dynasty, while our Imperial Japan here had adopted and improved the clean lines and clear efficiency of the earlier Song dynasty.

He, Kono, was a proponent of *Hokushin-ron*, the northern route of expansion; it was quite natural that Japan should annex large regions of northern China and eventually battle the Soviet Union for Siberia. Who knows, one might be able to occupy Alaska, too, and then push down to California.

Chaplin began by saying that China could only be

pacified by completely destroying the innumerable warlords, the Communists hadn't the slightest chance (here Amakasu squirmed inwardly at the actor's political dilettantism), Japan alone could still get a handle on the anarchic circumstances that had overrun large portions of Asia. And Chiang Kai-shek? Oh, the Kuomintang were weak and decadent, that was why Manchuria had been occupied after the Mukden Incident, to establish a new utopian interior, a resource-rich colony of dreams: Manchukuo, a counter-embodiment, so to speak, of the divine-imperial.

My, Chaplin was quite the little Japanese nationalist, Amakasu thought, which was obviously due to indoctrination by this Kono, you had to hand it to him. Live squid was served to a round of appreciative *ah*s and *oh*s, and the Italian colonel excused himself to visit the lavatory.

Having listened intently, Ida, the young German girl, wanted to remark that only the *Nanshin-ron*, the southern route of expansion, would lead Japan to success, when suddenly, as if something were blinding her, she jerked her hands to her face, too late! the sneeze had already worked its way loose from her face, blasting forward like a typhoon; a long, glistering drop dangled from her nose, reflecting not only the rice-paper walls of the private room and the warm yellow lamps on the ceiling, but also the appalled expressions of the Japanese in attendance.

Amakasu bit his lower lip to keep from bursting into laughter and slid his silken-socked foot farther under the table, inch by inch, until it touched her ankle, resting there, stroking her now with the tips of his toes.

Ida, in turn, did not recoil, let him continue his rubbing, my goodness, whatever was she doing? Chaplin and Kono had taken up a new topic, the other guests having already forgotten the sneeze so as not to have to keep feeling shame for the young German woman.

If we really wanted to understand a mystery, Amakasu said, smiling, the solution would appear from the matter itself, for answer and problem couldn't be separated from one another.

Obsequious waiters brought clay bowls of clear spring soup, a single, fragrant, early summer mushroom floating therein. Outside, far off on the slopes of Fuji-yama, it began to thunder.

Ida replied without hesitation that there was a forgetting of all existence, a falling silent of our being where we would feel as if we'd found everything. She looked him directly in the eyes while saying this, and Amakasu, his foot wandering gradually higher under the little table, was certain he had experienced this very exchange once before, he simply could not remember anymore when and where.

Their interest in the ascetic dance of dishes lost, the guests drifted over to the hotel ballroom little by little, dropping snatches of conversations behind them like wadded-up wastepaper. And then, beneath the modern chandelier, they moved somewhat bashfully to the jazz rhythms, the floor serving them as soundboard. Chaplin clapped his manicured hands while laughing with a trace of depravity.

When an Argentine tango was struck up, Amakasu grabbed the young German woman's hands and began to whirl her around—she was astonished at his virtuosity in dance, smiled; as they spun in circles, the light from the wall sconces streaked across her vision, and Amakasu dipped her elegantly to the floor. Whoops, could be that she had drunk too much rice wine.

22.

Tsuyoshi Inukai, Japan's prime minister, sends a messenger to invite his son Takeru Inukai, Charles Chaplin, and Masahiko Amakasu to dine with him this evening in his residence, if they so please.

For reasons that will never be adequately fathomed, this message does not reach Chaplin. So the prime minister sits at home humming quietly at the *chabudai*, that simple low table his grandfather bequeathed to him such a long time ago, and in gentle anticipation contemplates the garden, illuminated so softly by the room's lightbulbs, listening to the fresh trickles of a fountain outside.

When three quarters of an hour have passed, he flips open his pocket watch, sighs faintly, and, after instructing the servants to put away the two choice bottles of red wine and the crystal glasses, dismisses them, together with the security personnel, and they withdraw to the staff wing.

What has happened instead is that Chaplin is attending a Noh performance this evening along with Inukai junior and Amakasu. And now young naval cadets flit into the residence on sock feet to kill the prime minister and the actor, whom they likewise suppose to be present, since they are certain the superior national character of Japan, the *kokutai*, is threatened.

Chaplin is not there, oh, how maddening, so they set off a smoke grenade and put a revolver to the aged prime minister's chest. He manages to shout *If I were only free to speak the truth*, but they reply coldly *The time for talking has passed* and pull the trigger, once, twice, many times, *pop-pop-pop* it goes, as though unleashed, reckless Champagne corks were flying about; the prime minister is dead instantly, black smudges of gunpowder dust his white shirtfront, his beard is sticky with blood of a blackberry hue, like the dark remnants of a pudding.

Meanwhile, at the other end of the city, seated in the dimness of the Noh theater are: Takeru Inukai, Kono, Amakasu, Ida, and Chaplin, who has been informed in advance that the most artful stories in Noh lack both plot and representative characters and feature ghosts.

They all suspect nothing of the young military officers' coup attempt, outside the weeklong rain has stopped, and Ida, who has already attended several of

90

these performances, suddenly feels herself reminded of her hours with Ezra Pound, of her long-lost book on Noh, and then the first actor is already onstage, masked in red, draped in silken fabric, an iron ring atop his head, his hands painted red, accompanied by incisive, glittering flute melodies, and everything is forgotten in the spell of the events. It is now the hour that brings back longing . . .

> *It was the hour the sailor's tender heart,*
> *Beset by homesick urges, swims in yearning,*
> *That day in tears from loved ones e'er to part,*
>
> *That softly sets the novice pilgrim churning,*
> *When sounds of evening bells he hears afar*
> *Bewail a day to embers gently burning.*

Now Kono interrupts the freshness and purity of this melancholy moment (and notwithstanding the vastly higher-ranking prime minister's son beside him), lecturing at a whisper: the essential aspect of Noh theater is the concept of *jo-ha-kyū*, which states that the tempo of events is to begin slowly and auspiciously in the first act, the *jo*, then accelerate in the next act, the *ha*, and finally, in the *kyū*, reach its climax abruptly and as expeditiously as possible. Kindly pay attention to the actors, Kono says, see here, they must move across the stage like delicate ghosts, shuffling and sliding their feet without lifting them from the floor.

It is the tale of the *kanawa* being told there on the slightly elevated stage, the tale of the iron ring of jealousy. Look, the actor is holding the *hannya* to his face, the demon mask of a jealous woman.

During the reign of Tennō Saga, there lived a princess who loved to no avail, and at this she grew so furious with jealousy and grief that she went to the shrine in Kibune and prayed for seven days to become a *hannya*, a demon. On the seventh day the deity took pity and appeared to her, saying, *If you wish to become a* hannya, *you must go to the river Uji and lie there in the water for twenty-five days*. She did as she was told and afterward returned to Kyoto, overjoyed, and wove her hair into five strands and painted her face and her body red and placed on her head an iron ring with three candles affixed to it. And she put between her teeth a torch that burned at both ends. And when she went out into the streets, the people saw she was a devil.

And Amakasu, sensing something akin to an incorporeal and yet profound mental intimacy to Ida, clasps his hands together as if in prayer, ponders how he might later steer her to his futon, and after the show, which in fact, as prescribed by the *kyū*, ends surprisingly quickly, they escape into the street, where they hear that the prime minister has been killed and the famous American actor Charles Chaplin, too, although he is standing right there among them. Nodding bows to one another, they hail two taxis in faintly fluttering panic and ride home, anxious and taciturn; something altogether odd has happened.

23.

Nägeli, we recall, is traveling up to Germany in that rickety plane through the lard-gray murk over Lake Constance, in order to present himself at Universum Film AG in Berlin after having found absolutely no inspiration whatsoever in ossified Switzerland, Scandinavia, or France.

Those baleful premonitions that the plane might explode in midair from the detonation of a suitcase bomb dissolve in the very moment the clouds disperse, and he can make out below the light-beige, rectangular building blocks of Berlin Central Airport.

They circle in the air for a while, then fly a spiraling

loop in a downward hurtle (Nägeli's coffee slops out), touching down rudely—the wheels skip a few times before the aircraft safely taxis to a stop. He extends the cuff links of his dress shirt toward his nibbled fingernails as is his custom, grabs his little valise from the contraption, climbs down the stepladder, and hands his identification papers to the uniformed German waiting on the tarmac—who naturally does not return Nägeli's friendly smile.

They were going to entrust him here with a huge project, his secretary said in Zurich, a global project, Hugenberg, an obscene amount of money, German money, foreign money, maybe a hundred thousand dollars, God, he is vain enough. Marveling, he is chauffeured through the verdant streets; in the metropolis dated films like *Der Kongreß tanzt* haven't been screened for some time now, unlike in sleepy-town Zurich, but instead there are a number of brand-new, remarkable, formally absolutely radical pictures, announced in broad daylight by hypnotizing neon advertisements of gigantic proportions whose fleet runs of glowing light bite themselves in the tail; the flashing banners at left have hardly gone out before those at right begin again.

Precipitous, modern, jagged, the office building's

façade towers aloft; meanwhile he is kept waiting in the marbled atrium inside, draped in one of those German avant-garde, chrome-plated, black leather chairs, next to a withered potted palm. Over there: mirrored glass windows, statues in agate, a dull wisp of *Kölnisch Wasser*. Beside his seating area a red-liveried boy diligently operates the clicking buttons of a double-shafted elevator car; people hasten inside, harrumphing officiously, zooming upward.

This, now, is the epicenter of world cinema; everyone who is anyone is in Berlin, old and young alike: Wiene, Lang, Pabst, Boese, Sternberg, Riefenstahl, Ucicky, Dudow.

Nägeli suddenly feels the strong urge to comb his hair, arises, searches in vain for the washrooms, is confused and ill at ease, like someone who, in a bad dream, has become lost.

Just then an exuberant little blond man hurries toward him (double-breasted suit, pinstripes, Aryan midget), pumps both his hands rhythmically, assuring him of his deeply felt esteem for and his eternal friendship with the Swiss, his Helvetic brethren; this is a singsong, a chipper, smirking tumbling-out-and-about of courtesies, a bright boyish joyfulness on full display before him such that never would one ever suppose something else lay underneath, something darkly golden, proletarian, scheming.

Yes, yes, indeed, Nägeli's German is utterly flawless and unaccented, impeccable, he speaks it even better than the Germans do (*Haha! Guffaw!*), Nägeli—*oh, what nonsense*—Heinz will simply call him Emil; then Heinz Rühmann's forefinger curls, beckoning, producing now, Mephistopheles-like, a second German from behind a marble column, as though he had been hiding there in wait this whole time.

He, however, is the contrasting part of this double bill, the midnight showing: dark skin, dark-black, oily hair parted down the middle and spilling over his forehead, thuggish hands, a well-fitting suit, padded shoulders, tall, a big fellow, a house of a man, elegant, powerful, a golden signet ring on his pinky finger. His friends call this oaken hulk here Putzi, Putzi Hanfstaengl, Heinz laughs, and then: Putzi flings open his coat, twirls forth a pocket watch, flips it open with a circular motion, peeps at the clockface theatrically, his one eyebrow drawn up like Emil Jannings, what, my oh my, already half past two in the afternoon and everyone still sober, the three of them will have to treat themselves to some entertainment in Berlin (duskily Lower Bavarian, gutturally trilled *R*s in *three*, *treat*, and *Berlin*).

Nägeli demurs, he is too tired; Rühmann again, this time: *oh, what utter nonsense*, come along, Swiss, there's no getting out of this. But what about his appointment? Now listen here, double bow and scrape, *they* are his appointment, them, Heinz and Putzi, at your service!

24.

And so they ride together to a cabaret near Nollendorf-platz, in the cavernous spatial inscrutability of which scantily clad chorus girls are reflected on the walls. Champagne (a jeroboam): the glass table strains under its weight. Putzi's giant fingers remove a cigar's bande-role with such nimble tenderness; the syllables *ver-i-tas* twinkle silver in a pin on his lapel, ostentatiously proclaiming his membership in the Harvard Club. The revue girls whisper, giggle, Rühmann takes mischievous pleasure in being recognized, and, surprised at himself, Nägeli realizes he can't stand the two of them.

Thrust through a gap in the dark-blue velvet curtain, a face peers out, painted white with a thick paste, the middle of its lower lip alone highlighted by a bloodred dot. The curtain now opens completely, and the face acquires arms and legs, a stiff tailcoat appears, it is a skeletal master of ceremonies, who skillfully attracts the undivided attention of the hall to himself with one gloved gesture, then a little orchestral flourish, *silenzio*, darkness, a single yellow spotlight sets the man's patent leather shoes ablaze with light, stage smoke, at first scattered clicking, now a continually accelerating clacking, the man's rhythmically gamboling feet are turning into a typewriter, into machine-gun fire, and thus no one in the audience notices the arrival of Reich Minister Hugenberg, who, flanked by two or three slick and sluggish goons, has been waiting for precisely this moment of the performance to plop himself down in the sofa corner reserved for him.

Tanned an indecent nut brown from his Swiss ski vacation, owner and sole god of Universum Film AG, the most powerful man in German cinema, etcetera, etcetera—this is Hugenberg. Pistol grips can be seen peeking out from the unbuttoned suit coats of his escorts; one of them is even wearing the revolver stuck in his front waistband. Gangsters, mumbles drunk Nägeli.

And now an agent from Danish Nordisk is also there, someone Nägeli has never seen before but who addresses him familiarly in English (he signaled to Hugenberg after the latter's private screening of *Die Windmühle* that he could get that fellow Nägeli to show up in Berlin inside of a week; one just had to draw enough dollar signs in the air over the phone. Well, then get him up here, mewed a crapulous Hugenberg, who had drifted off during the film; tedious opening sequences had wandered through his mogulish synapses; colorless shadows, logs, coal ovens, disconsolate farm girls, Swiss ennui, a great deal of it), yet then yields to Hugenberg, who scoops his hefty hands toward Rühmann.

This fellow here, thin Heinz, blond Heinz, little Heinz, like the red tomato sauce, this, my dear Swiss friend, is the greatest comedic talent of the twentieth century aside from Chaplin.

At any rate, a film needs to be made with him, a comedy, Nägeli will fly to Japan with German Lufthansa (or travel by ship, whatever he likes), where he can reunite with his fiancée in Tokyo and then shoot a film there that will put everything that has ever been made to proverbial shame (Nägeli also ought to bear in mind his secret trip to Italian Somaliland, those film shoots there for Flaubert's *Salammbô* that were abandoned after a week, what a catastrophe, water under the bridge, not worth mentioning, wink, wink). Your associate Arnold Fanck has also been asked, it must be said in fairness, but he is rather more grounded in his work while you, my good Swiss, are a film director with his head in the heavens, the clear ether, the capricious froth of the sun, the shadows of the clouds, aren't you?

And then, without waiting for a reply, Hugenberg stands up, his legs splayed apart, swaying slightly as if he were a captain at sea, grows yet taller, puffs himself up, physically filling out the void his aura is projecting, stares at Nägeli, and thunders: Two hundred thousand dollars are completely at his disposal. He may pick his own topic, a Japanese-German film company is being established for him, he just has to make a movie, with Zeiss lenses, lord, yes, a sound film, whatever, our pal Rühmann here in the main role, everything is up for discussion, it doesn't even have to be a comedy, Nägeli can call all the shots.

Nägeli leans over the table to that indomitable man with the crew cut, gazes up at him, stunned, takes a gulp of the sparkling wine (one of the gangsters has inadvertently ashed in his glass); never before has he so vividly been served up the madness and megalomania of the Germans. Up onstage a slender elf haltingly loosens the brassiere from her boyish breasts.

Why? Why all this? The tycoon shakes with laughter, and it sounds like a rachitic goat. Why, indeed? Why, Hugenberg doesn't just want to snub the Americans, he wants to get out of the unbreachable contracts they've entered into with Paramount, then he of course wants to bring in the Japanese, who reject sound film and will sooner or later subdue the Asian continent, just imagine those gigantic markets, they can't simply be surrendered to Metro-Goldwyn-Mayer without a fight, the globe must be overrun with German films, colonized with celluloid. After all, film is nothing but cellulose nitrate, gunpowder for the eyes. Cinema, Hugenberg says, lighting one of Putzi's cigars, cinema is war by other means. Nägeli, flummoxed: everyone has gone insane.

And now Siegfried Kracauer turns up staggering, terrifically drunk, the head of the *Frankfurter Zeitung*'s culture section. He stumbles while shaking hands with Nägeli and Hugenberg and Putzi and Heinz—he is to convey best, sincere, warm wishes from Bloch and Benjamin (the irony dissipates unheard), soon he'll probably have to leave Germany, it's looking grim here, but at least there's still our brother Kästner over in Babelsberg who'll write *the best* screenplays—Hugenberg, who now no longer wishes to ignore this hostile tone, turns away in disgust.

Nägeli asks for a cigarette, whereupon he is handed a glass of warm, flat beer, the way Englishmen like to drink it, he knocks it back in a single swig, then another, now Putzi is ordering whiskey on top of that, then finally

Champagne once more, down the hatch with it, too, four glasses, two hundred thousand dollars. Oh, fair, drunken Germany, Nägeli thinks.

A smoking woman slinks up to the table imperiously and with great self-confidence, a film critic, Hooray, she shouts, but of course, certainly, she knows all of Nägeli's films, kudos, a pleasure, really, *Die Windmühle* being a thunderous masterpiece.

Then she performs some sort of coin trick, and while the orchestra launches itself from an appealing popular tune (during which the now stark-naked troupe of sprites leaves the nebulous stage, to the right and to the left, with astonishing dispassion) to the safety of a slightly stale tarantella, Kracauer elbows Nägeli in the side; that's Lotte Eisner, notorious for her ruthless hatchet jobs of films that surge against the rocks of her razor-sharp mind and are there adjudged bad or (even worse) insignificant. And Eisner, well, she winks at Nägeli, blowing him a kiss.

Putzi straightens his cuffs and tops up everyone's glass; a waiter invariably positioned at attention near the group is quickly chased off to fetch another bottle of Champagne. And now Lotte Eisner quite brazenly seizes the hand of the powerful UFA lord, gives it a squeeze, and says: There is no better filmmaker than that shy Swiss over there, how fortunate, no? that he is not a Jew.

Abashed silence, but faraway, dense Hugenberg is visibly stirred by this joke (which it is not) while the lickspittle from Nordisk, who has of course first waited for Hugenberg's reaction, eagerly and with a click of his heels raises his Champagne glass, and Heinz Rühmann breaks into a quite malevolent sneer. And lo: even on the countenances of the revolver men, fossilized for hours now, there appears the chaste hint of a smile.

25.

And Kracauer and Eisner (who, Nägeli notices in his inebriation, has a wonderfully pretty pursed mouth) — having finally given the slip to Hugenberg and his blond little monkey Heinz and Putzi the Golem at the Hotel Adlon around three thirty in the morning—now embark on a breakneck taxi ride with Nägeli, during the course of which he must request the vehicle be stopped at once, there, at the edge of the Tiergarten. Exeunt. The sky, it plunges upward, dark and starless.

Nägeli kneels down on one leg, retching and retching, while bracing himself on the black automobile's rear fender, his face contorted theatrically and illuminated in profile by the taxi's yellow taillights (as though he himself were suddenly starring in one of those garishly overblown, now slightly antiquated German films with overly mannered acting), then relief; he wipes his mouth with the back of his hand, Kracauer putting his arm around his shoulders warmly and amicably; they climb back into the car, and Lotte Eisner holds a vial of Hoffmann's anodyne under the nostrils of this slender Swiss soul.

And now it continues, this nocturnal swoon through Berlin, under the light of streetlamps blurred by intoxication, past soaring steel colossi, past dozens of clownishly made-up whores frozen in salacious poses on the curb, past shoeblacks, rat catchers, disabled bodies. Trucks, loaded with jeering youths racing from one political melee to the next, speed through red traffic lights.

And above them, yet again, as if they were driving in circles, shimmers the noxiously green neon-light ad of the Philips company, extolling the virtues of pentode tubes.

What nerve you had with this Hugenberg fellow, Nägeli says to Eisner. The truth is, she replies, we've got maybe another six months to live in Germany. At most. That's why it is essential not to engage in self-denial anymore, not for another minute.

Yes, that goes for him, too, Nägeli, Kracauer adds, a director should believe in the absoluteness of his subject, yes, yes, he must believe in vampires and in ghosts and in miracles. Only then would emerge, presto: Truth. Nägeli nods, swallowing down the acrid taste of what he has just vomited up; yes, they are right, his new friends.

Up front, the taxi driver then says something very ugly in cowardly grousing Berlin dialect: The Jews are to blame for the whole mess, for all of this. All the better if they are chased off, to Timbuktu, deep into the most distant jungle where those vermin belong. Whoever doesn't want to live like a respectable German here can simply get going, or get got, and he draws the edge of his hand across his gullet.

Nägeli wants to give him a smack from behind; Lotte holds on to his arm, it's better to just ignore these sorts of things, but then Kracauer, who is sitting up front next to the driver, pokes him in the eyes with two outstretched fingers, the chauffeur cries out, jerking his hands from the steering wheel to his face, and the now driverless Mercedes swerves to the left, just barely missing a car in the oncoming lane (the honking races past, as if they were seated in some diabolical sound tunnel, first directly in front, then from the side, finally from behind), avoids a stately chestnut tree on the left, on the right an oak; then the taxi smashes into an advertising pillar, and there it comes to rest, smoking and with a steam-sputtering, accordioned radiator hood, beneath one of those gaudily colored posters touting the rather untenable promises of Electoral List No. 2 (Bread and Jobs).

Nägeli and Eisner are heaved forward slightly, but aside from the bloody nose of Kracauer, whose fit of laughter reveals a row of teeth with blood from his mouth climbing up the gaps between them, no one has come to grief.

Two gendarmes who appear more at a saunter than at a run are handed dollar bills by Lotte Eisner; they disappear again (over at Nollendorfplatz there are more important matters anyway—a goon squad of recently banned Brownshirts has come upon a detachment of the likewise banned Hamburg Red Navy; blood is flowing there in much greater quantities), Kracauer gives the chauffeur, who now resembles a Teutonic, comedic Virgil cowering beside his battered taxi, a well-placed kick, they hasten down the boulevard, to the left, right, left again, more fits of laughter, more hugging, and then, in a conspiratorial flat on Tauentzienstrasse, on whose pale-green velvet wallpaper the first shudders of daybreak will soon tremble, the three lie recumbent on the rug before the hearth, smoking, and

Lotte and Siegfried are certain of having found in him the right one, and into the intimacy of this moment they plant the thought that Nägeli, whom they consider to be the very best, must make a horror film, an allegory, if you like, of the coming dread.

And Nägeli, who on the one hand sees flashing before him Hugenberg's two hundred thousand magical dollars (which are, alas, pegged to the requirement that he cast Heinz Rühmann) and on the other hand finds the gigantic irony of this idea downright wonderful, laughs, blowing smoke up at the ceiling, and the longed-for deliverance is here; the whole time he's thought he wouldn't let that blond cretin in front of his camera, and yes, that is exactly the idea that's been eluding him for months; he'll shoot a horror film, it just has to be made palatable to UFA somehow, he'll simply no longer mention Rühmann, yes, he'll go to Japan and film there—after all, he was invited, or so he understood Hugenberg earlier—everything will be paid for. And it's really quite obvious: the undead fiend in his film must be a good-looking, slim Asian man, which is to say, exactly the opposite of blond Rühmann.

Right, one just has to think big, everything else will take care of itself, Lotte Eisner giggles, opening another bottle of Champagne, and Kracauer, who has wandered off now into the kitchen to poach some eggs, calls back:

Why, of course, a woman could also play the part of the living dead, an Asian woman, Anna May Wong, for example, then you'd be rid of Rühmann permanently. His eggs do not turn out, so he simply beats another half dozen into the skillet and in no time carries the omelet into the salon, impishly whistling *The Internationale*.

Two hundred thousand isn't nearly enough, you really have to fleece the Reich, Nägeli must meet Hugenberg again and demand three, oh, why not? four hundred thousand to fulfill UFA's fantasies of world domination. But that's a gigantic scam, Protestant Nägeli protests, he's never done anything like this before, nor does he have any ideas, at which Lotte interjects, it's the others who are dishonest, the *furschlugginer* Reich ministers, the purveyors of culture, the capitalist profiteers, yes, even the journalists who support this glaring corruption and this brutish power structure, who support the pandering and preservation of their skittishly defended economic security with their irrelevant, mediocre scribblings.

She could just vomit, vomit, if it weren't so sad. Kracauer smiles and gently touches Eisner's arm. At some point the birds begin their song outside, and the discussions melt away, becoming softer and one with the rising arpeggio of the early morning street noise.

And so it happens that Nägeli, after having slept

facedown for eight hours on Kracauer's sofa without moving a muscle, his head howling needles, casually telephones Hugenberg's office, requests an appointment, and even keeps it that afternoon, too, despite his Swiss conscience's suggestion that he not go through with it for heaven's sake and instead hurry back to his safe Zurich, there's still time, last chance not to agree to this misplaced Faustian pact, everything can still be broken off helter-skelter, *basta*, *bupkes*, *finito*, *finale*. But of course he does end up going to Hugenberg's office. On his way there, untold numbers of swastikas line Berlin's façades; like mindless swallows they hang there.

26.

Chaplin more or less forced Amakasu to hold this press conference, for which over a hundred journalists—the entire regiment of international writers accredited in Japan and their photographers—now gather in the ball-room of the Imperial Hotel, which has been comman-deered expressly for this purpose. The French are there, the Italians, the Swedes, the Russians, the Americans of course, and the Germans, then Chinese, easily a dozen Englishmen; there is simply no end to the upraised steno pads, the sketching draftsmen, and the popping bursts of flashbulbs.

They have, as always, agreed on English as a mediating language, and dim-witted, indeed almost impertinent, questions tumble through the room. Is there now, in his opinion, a power vacuum in Tokyo, did the young officers act on their own, how exactly did Chaplin escape the assassination attempt, has the film star now armed himself in anticipation of further attempts on his life, and if so, with what? Does he own a revolver? If so, what make? Will Chaplin now leave Japan with unpleasant impressions of the country? They of course wouldn't be able to hold it against him—whom they erroneously insinuate to be an American—but didn't one also have to say in fairness that the murder attempt was directed more at him as a symbol, at the Little Tramp, at the silhouette of an actor, and not at him personally?

While the questions rain down upon Chaplin, he seeks to find a line between sensitive Englishman and bumbling likeable figure; it would perhaps be incorrect to say that he is fidgeting around; just because he is grimacing and gesticulating about and daubing his forehead doesn't mean he isn't relying on the impact of his charm, perfected over the course of what feel like centuries of public appearances; coquettishness also belongs to his repertoire, an ostensible shyness, evasion. And the journalists buy it, this able performance of the idiot savant; in the end what is he even supposed to say about it anyway? He is an actor, and the exquisite byzantinisms of Japanese statecraft remain for him as arcane as the complexities of his Swiss wristwatch. Besides, he is drunk, again.

Amakasu sits next to him, smiling stonily, half turning back time and again to the two Foreign Ministry officers flanking him, feeling that if he does not move aside fast enough they will stab him from behind the next moment or loop a garrote around his neck, put a foot into the small of his back, and shout *Ten thousand years! Banzai!*

Images from a waking dream of recently experienced indignities appear, and although he bridles at their manifestation, they are as palpable and real as this room full of journalists and the officers standing behind him.

The invitation to dinner from a family of aristocrats close to the emperor, which he was of course simply delighted to accept, the offer to sit at the prince's table, to the left of His Highness himself, even though the seat should actually have gone to those of higher rank—despite his more humble origins Amakasu had finally felt he had arrived.

He had chatted with refined politeness and elegance as the servants whisked around him; the others had, or so he thought, enjoyed his company, asking him for his opinion, which he had revealed to them drop by drop, politely masked, admittedly, as befitting the occasion and the guests. It had been a glorious evening, and he had returned to his ordinary home euphoric and in high spirits.

Two weeks later he had been invited there once more; filled with anticipation, he had a servant show him from the villa's entrance to his seat, which, however, was now located at the farthest imaginable chair from the prince, between a rubber trader from Indochina and a bespectacled, hirsute Greek danseuse who had obviously seen better days.

Try as he might, he was unable to fathom what he could have done wrong; it was as if someone had switched off the sun. The dinner discussions proceeded sluggishly and laboriously, and the prince, who at the previous supper had virtually paid court to him, not only ignored him completely, but had, it seemed, even instructed the other guests to avoid him as conspicuously as though he had been stricken all of a sudden by a disfiguring and contagious ailment. Even the rubber trader evaded his verbal advances. He was never invited back.

When the press conference is finally over, he still feels shame at this agonizing memory. His ears seem a few degrees warmer than the rest of him. He exhales audibly.

The two officers, as it turns out, are not assassins at all, and instead escort him and Chaplin to the door of the Imperial Hotel, through the throng of journalists still photographing with enthusiasm, and into a waiting limousine, and one of them, a young lieutenant with almost transparent jug ears, grazes his sleeve, bows deeply, and says he has such great esteem for Chaplin, would it perhaps be possible for him, Amakasu, to ask for his autograph, it's for his young daughter, of course only if it doesn't cause all too great a fuss.

27.

Deposited in Hugenberg's outer office by the secretary,
a shrew as coarse as she is sturdy (she orders him to sit
and wait on a chair in the middle of the room as though
he were an improper little lapdog to be punished),
Nägeli rolls a pale-violet pencil (which had materialized there through the ether from God knows where)
back and forth on the floor with his shoe, looks at his
watch, searches in vain for an ashtray, pockets the pack
of cigarettes again, glances at his watch once more
when, after five or six minutes that stretch out like
chewing gum, the double doors open and the tycoon
appears, blustering up a grin, his arms flung apart, his
palms gaping as wide as shovels for a welcoming
embrace.

Whiskey glasses are filled, ice cubes tossed in with
a *clink*, oil paintings on the walls of his titanic office
pointed at: Voilà!—Ingres, Gros, Delacroix, de Neu-
ville, yes, only the French are able to paint war appro-
priately, just look at that, goddamn, how precisely that's

done, those muscular, bleeding flanks of the fatally wounded horse on the battlefield at Borodino.

And Nägeli absorbs everything in its pathetic, vulgar excess. There is a white porcelain jaguar ready to pounce, as tall as a man. And a modern rug embroidered in nightmarishly garish hues. And a little black cat trying with piteous mewls to induce the door of a grotesquely oversized refrigerator to open by scratching at it.

Through picture windows one has a view far out onto Berlin. Nägeli suppresses an incredible yawn, attempts to subdue the pounding in his head, only partly looks and listens, examines the ice in his glass, recognizing in the vanishing frosty cubes by turns shamrocks, top hats, tears, the syllables *ver-i-tas*, as if it were dawning upon him that this frosty, inverted reiteration of the molybdomancy familiar to him from his childhood was in fact, by virtue of how melting liberated the form, the ideal reduction of memory.

He silently curses his new friends Kracauer and Eisner for having persuaded him to prostitute himself here before this braggart who, on top of everything else, also suffers from being a rich parvenu—the only things still missing are the golden eating utensils. However does he leave here again with his self-respect intact?

And now Hugenberg, chattering away nonstop,

seats himself at the eagle-footed grand piano, flips up some imaginary coattails, and with unsightly enthusiasm plays *Ein Freund, ein guter Freund*, the frayed cigar hanging from his mouth the whole time, unlit, and, underfoot, his silk socks are tucked into velvet slippers monogrammed in gold, and in the corner the cat is squalling.

Nägeli feels like a canary in a coal mine, awaiting the poisonous fumes. This is simply the most egregious lack of probity, as if this were all just a game, a circus attraction, a masquerade, as if there were not hundreds of thousands of dollars at stake, just play money from a dollhouse, from a toy shop made of paper, this Zampanò Hugenberg, this puppet theater, this operetta, this buffoonery; hanging above him is the painting of a nude odalisque engaged in a staring contest with her friend, a skeleton.

Nägeli speaks very quietly and guardedly of his filmic plans. He would really prefer that no one heard them. All the while Hugenberg raps on a high key with a forefinger swollen like a stuffed sausage, *plink*, *plink*, *plink*, always the same note.

He wants to shoot a horror film? And do it all in Japan? Lips are pursed, bristly hair scratched, monocle jammed in eye and twisted out again, Nägeli, expecting to be thrown out immediately, takes a step backward toward the outer office, but Hugenberg raises his hand.

Stop! Well, well. A bold idea. By all means. He was most favorably impressed by *Shanghai Express*. And boldness impresses him, too. And for an Asian thriller one absolutely needs boldness by the bucketful. He likes it, he likes it. Has Nägeli already thought of Anna May Wong? But hold on, it simply won't work at all for Rühmann to act, too. How would that even look, a short blond like him among all those yellow people?

Nägeli tries to banish all emotions from his face, but he does not need to; the dreadful man has hit on it, all by himself. Everything is of course going to be much, much more expensive, Hugenberg now says, puffing, two hundred thousand dollars won't even come close to covering it.

So let's get around to the screenplay first. He's heard his fiancée is already in Japan? Well then, she could—assuming she's blonde (Nägeli nods, smoking, examining his gnawed fingertips)—play the oh-so-chaste girl who must be protected from the depravity of the undead.

He's thinking of Bram Stoker and *Otranto* and *Nosferatu* and so forth, sulfurous fumes, the young mademoiselle will naturally be bitten on the throat before she can be brought to safety. This is all construed narrowly and simply, there aren't any grand options here; it needs evil on the one hand, sexually charged of course—Aryan innocence will be corrupted by the Asian beast (naturally it mustn't be phrased like *that* to our Japanese friends)—and on the other hand there's got to be an adversary for the undead antagonist who subjects him to the bright morning light at the end and kills him with, how could it be otherwise? a yew stake through the heart.

Yes, of course, Nägeli lies, out of his depth, that's roughly the film he's envisioning, but Ida, she can't act at all, and anyway: How can an aesthetic standard be applied to this? What Hugenberg is suggesting, after all, is just parody, or at best homage.

Oh, patience. And above all intuition. He'll figure it all out on his own, don't worry. One has to listen to one's inner voice, it'd be enough if he dipped his fingertips into the ocean of consciousness. Horror stories are universal, they're all very much alike, it's just a matter of variations on a theme. But what is he saying! Nägeli is the genius, after all, he's the one who enjoys his fullest confidence, isn't that so?

All right, brass tacks: a half a million dollars are available to him, even Fritz Lang wouldn't drum up that much these days after the *Metropolis* fiasco, Nägeli shouldn't mull it over all too long because tomorrow the war chest might be shut again or, rather, might be opened elsewhere. Off the record: one portion's from the Cinecittà and has to go back there, but what's gone isn't so easy to return, so this isn't theft per se, but might instead be called relocation—*Mysteries of the Economy*, Nägeli, right?

So, do they have an agreement? The fallboard of the piano is clapped shut to no applause, the masticated cigar laid not inelegantly on the edge of the instrument, the assistant barked in, she sails up among fluttering stacks of paper, a signature here, there, there, and here, and one more down there, no, at the very bottom right, please.

Why don't we add more to the bargain: *Eight* hundred thousand should suffice, no? And quite entre nous: Those Semites Kracauer and Eisner, they aren't really part of his circle of friends, one does need to stick together a little more among Nordic types, doesn't one? Exclusion is the magic word! Beware! And now: Champagne! And then: Time to leave, there's the exit! He has four other appointments this evening.

And while Nägeli totters out of the building after an elevator ride that lasts forever (but where, lonely, dying father, is he supposed to focus his *imawashii* gaze?), sinks down into the seats of the waiting limousine, and vows to himself never to drink alcohol again in this lifetime (in the car, the residual exhalations from the chauffeur's

119

hurriedly trodden-out cigarette smell terribly unappe-
tizing), Hugenberg is standing upstairs at his picture
window, legs astraddle, bellowing at his secretary that
he will certainly not be sending a German director to
those perverts in Japan, however unimportant he may
be—that'll be the day—they're just going to have to
make do with this Swiss dullard, have fun with *him*,
and close the door if you would.

And then he gazes out for a long while at the darkening metropolis below, and he sees before him that bi-
zarre film, that documentation of death mailed to him
from Japan, a flick that made him feel both pathos and
arousal, and he cocks his head slightly, running his fingers through his bristly hair, and grins like the nasty
swine he is.

28.

In the late afternoon Lotte and Siegfried board the
night train to Paris from Lehrter Bahnhof with two or
three suitcases in tow, in them the two little rolled-up
Kandinskys, a few books, the long linen nightgown

that belonged to Kracauer's grandmother, some dried flowers, cigarettes, toothbrushes. A bundle of dollar bills wrapped in a rubber band is tucked into Lotte's stockings.

In the darkening club car they bid farewell to their Germany and drink sweet cider and do not speak of memory tattering before them. Whoever has not left his homeland in grief and fear cannot know how they feel and how sorry they are, not ever.

At the French border in the dwindling light of early summer, they are waved through without further ado while other passengers are brusquely ordered into a wooden shed beside the tracks for further examination. No, their passports are in order, they needn't produce their suitcases, the border patrol salutes them with two fingers to the uniform cap, then everyone is boarding again, a solitary whistle, hissing wheelworks, onward.

Now, suddenly, sitting at the opposite table, across the aisle, is Fritz Lang, likewise en route to Parisian exile with a copy of *The Testament of Dr. Mabuse* in his luggage, as if a weary demiurge had devised this to be just so—and thus Lang is sitting on the same train in a yellow scarf, in the same club car even, and at this act of providence all seems like a new beginning.

They take seats together straightaway, huddling up, smoking, calling for two bottles of red wine, for salty snacks, cocktail pickles, pearl onions, should they have any on board. My goodness, he really must finally tell of the debacle. Sure, gladly. Well, so, Thea of course stayed in Berlin, she made her choice, for Burgundy, as she put it, and Fritz was welcome to defect to Etzel's dread encampment; and Lang, who rarely mixes art with life—but just this one time does—told her softly that she ought to know then who sets themselves on fire at the end.

Thea was still cursing after him in the stairwell, and then she was standing on the balcony of their large flat at the corner of Ku'damm, her slender arms wrenched aloft, the taxi had already driven up, and she shrieked down a shrill cry of rage and horror about how he was actually making it come true, but Lang wasn't listening anymore. She could keep slavishly kneeling before Hugenberg for all he cared.

Lotte drains her glass in one approving gulp and tells Lang, who of course was lying a bit, about Emil Nägeli, who through some chicanery has been shipped off to Japan, and Lang, who regards *Die Windmühle* as one of the most important films of all time and Nägeli as a gigantic talent in a Switzerland not exactly amply endowed with great artists, does not quite understand what the plan was exactly, except that UFA has been cheated, which of course suits him quite nicely.

Will Nägeli ever return, though? He's neutral by birth, says Siegfried, which is why those imminent sinister upheavals in Germany won't have any bearing on him, although on the other hand, Switzerland, at least the German-speaking part, will also be drawn into the new power brokers' sphere of influence by personages like that unsavory Gustloff.

Oh, luckily Paris is completely safe, my friends, smiles Lang, and Kracauer, who is already a great deal more inebriated than is good for him, replies that he's so very much looking forward to exile, and it's really quite splendid that they'll be living in the cradle of civilization from now on, in the *contrat social*, and not in that ghastly, bloody Berlin morphologically characterized by meat (and in particular: by *sausage*).

Besides, he didn't even bother to give notice for the flat on Tauentzienstrasse, just tossed the key into the mailbox. The furniture matters to him not a whit, the landlord can keep it or sell it as he likes; even so, he's just the very tiniest bit sorry about the Biedermeier secretaire, whereas the books can all be replaced.

Outside the train windows, French hamlets bathed in yellow light whizz by like beehives tended at night, pollinated only by the rushing of the railroad as it races past.

And forests! How differently, Lotte laughs, French

trees do breathe, how those oaks outside, blurred by the speed of the night train, are free from that Teutonic blather about their German soil beyond the border just crossed, German soil that murmurs so magically, that squeezes allegedly Druidic energy up into their branches, that once even showed the Caesars how the heathen, chthonic principle of the Stag King expresses victorious strength, that could vanquish Latin decadence with the mossy strength of Germania's primeval forests of oak. *Mon Dieu!*

Here's to that, says Lang, taking a sip of the club car wine and, soliloquizing and amused at himself, yanking his monocle out: I am now no longer Fritz Lang, I have crossed the border into exile and am Victor Hugo! Give me the Parthenon, the Alhambra, Notre-Dame, the Great Pyramid, the Uffizi Gallery, the porcelain towers of Esfahān; give me the Hagia Sophia, Borobudur, the Kremlin, El Escorial; give me cathedrals, mosques, pagodas; give me Phidias and Bashō, Dante and Aeschylus, Shakespeare and Lucretius, the Mahabharata and Job and Thoreau; give me the forests of France, the beaches of Indochina, the vast red plains of Ethiopia, the verdant hills of Connemara; give me a swarm of butterflies, the sea eagles over Alaska, the Sahara with its scorpions, Paris with its people; give me the Andes, the Pacific Ocean, a man, a woman, a gray-beard, a child, the blue sky, the dark night, the timid minuteness of the hummingbird, the immensity of the constellations; it is all good; I like it all; I have no preference in ideal nor in infinitude. But don't give me any more of this Heidelberg and Bach!

During this drunken philippic, Lotte and Siegfried squirm about in their seats; it is almost insufferable. They have no inkling that Lang will shuttle back and forth between Paris and Berlin for an entire year afterward, carefully balancing out whether maybe something might perhaps be worked out with UFA after all.

And so they smile bravely and sympathetically at Lang; God knows there are worse things than a temporary mental breakdown owing to their hurried getaway. The club car waiter has ducked out of sight so there is no more wine, and after a spell of further banter—during which certainly not a word is spoken about opportunism—they jerkily reach the first bleak suburbs of Paris, three Germans without their Germany.

29.

Many, many years, indeed, half an eternity later, a hulking giant dressed in black trudges across the snow-covered courtyard of his prison and clenches his frosty paws together. Underneath the wooden outhouse he has just exited, the urine he passed has long since frozen into a little yellow crystalline stalagmite. It is too cold for the birds, it is too cold to breathe, it is minus thirty-three degrees Fahrenheit in Iroquois Falls, Ontario.

Ernst Putzi Hanfstaengl, interned in Camp Q (Monteith) in the rather inhospitable part of northern Canada, yanks open the wooden door to the shelter with worn, good-for-nothing leather gloves, slams it shut behind him with a bang, shattering icicles, takes a seat right next to the pathetically small woodstove, and writes a long letter to James Bryant Conant, president of his alma mater, Harvard, wherein he complains about the conditions of his imprisonment and requests to be sent, when convenient, *a pair of heavy black oxfords, size 15D.*

Conant, who has been a vehement detractor of the new German regime since the early thirties, crumples up the letter unread, not even especially incensed about it—at most, irritated about Hanfstaengl's chutzpah at writing *him*, of all people, from the camp.

In any event, Putzi writes a great deal of letters, some to England, to Argentina, to his friend Charles Chaplin, and to the chairman of the Hasty Pudding Club, the solicitant, almost mendicant contents of which (he needs a piano more than anything) are reviewed by the Canadian military censor, blacked out in a few places, and then properly forwarded on. Mostly he reports for work duty in the nearby forest.

A Viennese inmate with whom he has become friends gives him a red-and-black plaid Mackinaw jacket of heavy wool, which is supposed not only to keep him warm, but also to help him stand out while felling trees, because of its high color contrast, and not be shot inadvertently by trappers. Putzi is thankful to the extent that this is possible for him. During his internment he has cried at night only once.

Amid the silent solitude of hard labor at the tree trunks, he is told the wolves will be coming down farther south than usual this winter, and after sunset at three or three thirty, he is frightened to hear them howling on the other side of the frozen lake.

He is friends with the guards, as much as one can be; they sometimes slip him chocolate, once even a dried sausage, but Putzi has lost forty or fifty pounds, his chubby cheeks have grown taut, and from time to time, in the evening, he lays his last pair of black silk socks neatly beside one another on his humble bed, next to the stained, dog-eared score of the *Goldberg Variations*, and he gently strokes them flat.

Perhaps he ought to try to escape, he must certainly still have friends on the West Coast, and from Vancouver he could either head down toward California and then to Mexico, or just stay on Victoria Island in that forlorn wooden cabin in Dollarton, with the Lowrys, whom he still knows from London—but how to traverse this immense continent unrecognized and without being followed? He will have to wait for summer, or at least until May.

One evening around six o'clock—it is still the miserably cold month of March and snowing exorbitant flakes outside again—after the few warmer days of a false spring have deceived him with their hopeful mirth, he pulls off the boots and socks he has been trying to jury-rig with newspaper insulation the whole winter long, inspects his malodorous feet (three of his toenails have already fallen off), and discovers on the side of his right big toe the inflamed beginnings of frost-induced gangrene.

He swears aloud in fear, slips back on his boots, which have essentially never deserved that name, and clomps out into the prison courtyard. The camp physician is only there two days a week; Putzi has long forgotten whether today is Tuesday or Thursday.

Light is still shining from the barracks of the infirmary, and music is playing on the radio. An armed guard greets him in passing; he raps on the wooden doors with his knuckles and enters without waiting for a response.

Dr. Lyle Bland lowers his newspaper and sighs, gazing up at Putzi with eyebrows raised, resignedly expecting another of Putzi's innumerable suadas, but this Putzi merely wordlessly sheds the heavy wool jacket and then the right boot, clonks his gigantic naked dirty foot onto the stool, and points at his toe, there, at the spot that has grown hard and dark and feels numb.

So you've come to me because of this measly thing, Dr. Bland says calmly, and Putzi, who has always gone rather meek when someone behaves with quiet authority and confidence, shrinks down a few millimeters to a more bearable level of boastfulness.

The camp doctor examines the toe, bending it back

and forth, tickles the shaded spot by gently rolling along its side his pale-violet pencil, and then on a loose slip of beige paper notes down with the same writing utensil that Putzi is exempted from forest labor until the spring and until that time is to receive double the wood ration for his stove. If it were to get worse, we'd need to operate, but for now we don't.

There. Satisfied? And now good night to you, *Jerry*. Something else? Yes! Here it goes, and the physician glances first at his fingernails and then at his wrist-watch: Putzi doesn't want to grow old and rot away here in this icy wasteland, he refuses to indulge these impositions, he is an intellectual who did, please note, defect at the right time, and a doctor like Bland must be able to comprehend this. While his detention might be legal, it is, however, not in the least morally defensible; the Allies have apparently forgotten that *he* had always warned against that Charlie Chaplin–esque demagogue, that irascible, drug-addicted, vulgar buffoon, whereas the Allies, meanwhile, had arranged themselves in their undiscriminating, black-and-white shadow cabinet where every German was equally guilty; they must lock all of them up without exception—so goes the hapless conclusion of such reasoning—whereas he's a decent man who desires nothing more than a quiet, reclusive life in the countryside, where it's warm of course, with the option of being useful to his fellow man. Nature, work, quiet, books, Johann Sebastian Bach, love of one's neighbor—that's his idea of happiness. And—is he supposed to be able to live like that here in Iroquois Falls, at the edge of the Arctic? Where his fucking toes are falling off? And while he's thinking about it, did he already mention the piano that should kindly be made available to him?

Dr. Bland gingerly slips the boot over the outstretched sock donned again after the examination and signals to the still incessantly grumbling Putzi, that's enough now, he may get up, please, and leave the infirmary through that door there.

The German does as he is ordered and scuffles out into the darkness of the snowy yard, dejected. Dragging along his supposedly diseased foot behind him like Mephistopheles's hoof, he disappears into his barracks while the doctor again attends to the radio receiver, a cucumber sandwich, and a glass of whole milk. Finland has surrendered to the Soviets.

30.

After the steamer docks in Kobe Harbor, few lasting images are impressed on Emil Nägeli's shadow-tendriled retinas (grayish gulls on the pier, construction rubble from a recent earthquake, two infirm, mumbling beggar monks, and the bloodied, vivid redness of raw slices of fish). The Towa Film Corporation representative sent to meet him—and who speaks outstanding German—performs a veritable St. Vitus's Dance of bows before him, then he boards the railroad to Tokyo, to his Ida.

Together they sink down, *osuwari kudasai*, into the cloud-like seats of a very elegant compartment, clearing their throats, cleaning their respective spectacles (with lightly pursed lips Nägeli aspirates a vaporous *O* over his double lenses), and adjusting their ties, and the Japanese man smooths his short, slightly obscene mustache with forefinger and thumb.

Well, *tsk-tsk*, conversation just doesn't want to get

moving; he feels as though his counterpart is waiting with some degree of laboriously concealed tension for Nägeli, who ranks far higher in the present compartment hierarchy, to please lead the discussion and, as it were, to set the right tone (the unuttered sound of the syllable *tō* meanwhile fills his mind with ineffable, dark promise). With his hand over his mouth, he suppresses a gas cloudlet pushing up his esophagus—that may very well be the raw fish, that brown sauce served with it, the green horseradish.

And so, with a superficiality that causes him to wince a bit, Nägeli lectures for a good three quarters of an hour on European cinema (while outside the windows of the zooming train Fujiyama moves past: quietly trembling, humming god-mountain), and lo and behold, the matter of rank having been satisfied, the young man waxes eager to give the honored guest the feeling with nods and smiles that his insights are not only of great interest, but also in fact thoroughly inspiring.

How tedious these triple contortions are, Nägeli thinks to himself, yet they are also the mark of an advanced civilization that expresses itself at once with extreme artifice and with the greatest naturalness. Another long silence ensues. As they look out the window into the sun, the young Japanese man noisily unscrews a thermos, peeps inside, and twists it shut again.

It crosses Nägeli's mind that he will have to learn to unfurl banalities not innate to his—ahem—Swiss spirit, to reel off formulas. Oh, the temperatures here in Japan are pleasant indeed, he, Nägeli, is rather surprised, one has seasons here like at home: autumn leaves, snowstorms, torrid summers. Yes, he continues, while suppressing a yawn, it is likely that only civilizations located in temperate climes are permitted to rise in splendor and renown; those in tropical zones foster in their people a lethargy that ensures no cultural foundations of relevance or duration can emerge, much less one with an imperial character. It tweaks him inside, this rubbish.

But—but what then of the pyramids of Mexico or Egypt or the remarkable achievements of the Khmer or even the Javanese, the young man argues, and Nägeli immediately realizes that the man is objecting more emphatically than decorum should allow; he sees how he bites himself hard on the lower lip, probably tasting some blood in his mouth.

He hastens to accept a cigarette from Nägeli's proferred silver etui, holds it in thanks up to his forehead in the Oriental manner, welcomes the Swiss gentleman's match with a nod, and pushes dragons of smoke from his nostrils. Just how to atone for this horrible tactlessness?

A white-gloved conductor appears, opens the compartment door, bows, and examines the tickets. The clicking of the train on the tracks grows louder and more relentless. Nägeli gnaws at one of his fingertips. No further conversation takes place. The Japanese man seems to feel dreadfully ashamed; he smokes and looks down at the floor. Finally, when this silence can scarcely be endured any longer, the train pulls into Kōjimachi District and, braking long and clamorously, comes to a stop at Tokyo's Central Station.

Luggage is loaded on and off, smartly coiffed men in dark suits, impatiently smoking, shove past women in forbidding kimonos whose cheeks—how fascinating to look at!—are covered in a pale paste and then highlighted with rouge. Nägeli's gaze tracks the hands on the face of a railway clock that glide toward one another in artificially slowed acceleration, only to unite then above at the capricious curvature of the twelve. A honking, a glinting, the flapping of pigeon wings, voices over the loudspeaker.

They have scarcely escaped that luminous cavern of a train station when the young Japanese man maneuvers the suitcase into a waiting taxi and orders the uniformed driver to take the most honorable foreigner to a certain address in Akasaka District, the trip shouldn't last even twenty-five minutes. Bows upon bows follow, which Nägeli still sees performed continually through the black-rimmed oval of the rear window even though the one thus bowing grows steadily smaller and more indistinct.

31.

Now and again during the ride, Nägeli captures these delightful scenes with his hands forming a rectangle, camera-like, before his eyes: soft sunlight at midday and bustling streets; fashionably clad youths (perfunctorily knotted, colorfully striped bow ties there, here bonbon-colored knit sweaters, white, loose knickerbockers) loiter about ice cream parlors; the iron wheels of streetcars, guided by gleaming tracks, screech away beneath telephone poles that march forth into the distance; tofu peddlers push their wooden carts against the current of hundreds of swarming bicyclists, tooting on the oca-rina flutes of their guild.

And here a small collision has taken place: an inattentive merchant has wheeled his trolley in front of an approaching truck, which was only partly able to brake, and now blood is gushing from the poor man's mouth, and he sits cowering on the cobblestone curb in shame and misery and weeping for his smashed tofu cart. A bespectacled police officer disperses the congregated masses with conciliatory gestures.

Tokyo is an electrifying polyphony of modernity and at the same time very, very ancient, a city that seems perfectly free of the taint of vulgarity. Filing past Nägeli's side window: stately women promenading emotionlessly in the shade of two parasols; wistful gingko trees, nestled against primeval stone bridges, arranged to such a degree of perfection that it seems as if they had been posed there by an artist; the bespectacled constable from a moment ago now regulating traffic stoically and stonily and myopically with raised white cuffs; then a military parade, on account of which the taxi must turn and take another route down and then right back up a gorgeous boulevard; as in a daydream they sail off underneath a delicate canopy of blossoms aglow in purple.

A breathlessness suffuses him, he loves what he sees, he could definitely stay here and create something. Yes, one aspect of his being feels itself continually reminded in Japan of something long forgotten that he cannot have experienced himself, an altogether intangible sensation of satisfaction enfolds him; delicious the way that bundle of telephone cables droops there in the middle; how a barber, comb in the pocket of his smock, tentatively steps out upon the threshold of his shop and yawns behind an upheld hand; the way an embarrassed crowd scatters off after there has been another small, unremarkable automobile accident; Nägeli scours his teeth with the tip of his tongue; they are covered by a thin bacterial film.

He feels something under his shoe, looks down to the floor of the taxi, and gropes for it. It is a pencil, a pale-violet one someone has left there. He rolls the clicking facets of the octagonal shaft in his hand and slips it into his blazer pocket as if he could somehow sense the mnemonic context and wished to keep the pencil only until he remembered what was meant by it.

Switzerland and its parochial clusters of mountains, those massifs jagged with the mere pretense of loveliness, have morphological repercussions on the ghastly orneriness of its citizens, who lean out their kitchen windows with elbows propped on a pillow to note down in pencil if someone has parked illegally in their neighborhood—which is to say, to write down the license plate number in order to report the driver later to the cantonal police. But even these pendants are never as bad as the Swiss creative class, whose dim and petty attitudes make him flee his homeland as often as humanly possible.

He must come up with something new, something completely unprecedented, it must be flawed, yes, exactly that is the essential factor; it is no longer enough to want to create a transparent membrane through film that might grant *one* of a thousand viewers the ability to perceive the dark, wonderful, magical light behind things. He must create something both supremely artificial and self-reflexive. That drunken vision that appeared to him so many weeks ago in Berlin with Kracauer and Eisner had revealed to him a new way forward, but now he must actually produce something full of pathos, must make a film that is recognizably artificial and deemed by audiences to be mannered and, above all, out of place.

It'd still be a horror film; one just couldn't depict creepiness with the clichés that horrible Hugenberg had preformulated for him in his glass poseur's office in Germany. And there won't be any vampires, nor any depraved, degenerate Asians, and most certainly not any young German women who allow themselves to be corrupted. Rather, Nägeli thinks, he has to devise a metaphysics of the present, in all its facets, from the innards of time outward. He'd still have to ponder it for a while, but then he'll know how to begin, in a few days, perhaps even by tomorrow.

The taxi turns off onto a side street, and Nägeli asks the driver, gesticulating, to please pull over on the left and wait for a moment. He climbs out, steps onto the sidewalk, bobbing up and down, and smokes a cigarette. Then he takes off his hat and with mild disapproval checks his appearance in the car's side mirror. The chauffeur grips the steering wheel with both white-gloved hands and out of cautiously expectant propriety keeps his eyes fixed straight ahead without turning back to Nägeli.

An airplane flies low past him in the sky; its cheerful drone, coupled with the twittering of birds in a nearby hedge, triggers a vibrant chain of memories that, as so often they do, send him falling down into the long-submerged world of his childhood. He sees before him the driver's white gloves resting on the steering wheel left and right, which in their furtive patience recall for him Sebastian, his little albino rabbit, whose fur was flayed as in Chinese torture, and at this moment he feels as though he could, for a short while, borrow the anguish of the world and its cruelty and turn it upside down, and transform it into something different, something good and true, as though he might possibly heal with his art.

32.

Thinking he might want to smarten himself up a bit before meeting his fiancée (and somewhat bewildered at this idea), Nägeli has himself deposited at a hair salon and enters the establishment. Inside he allows an ascetic-looking, inexorably humming hairdresser to shave his head with hair clippers. Then from a glass wall cabinet he selects—from among so many other wigs slyly awaiting their new purpose, like black scalps in a museum exhibit—a specimen made from dark-brown human hair.

While still in the shop (its chinoiserie wallpaper reminds him of those faintly dusty foyers in Swiss provincial theaters) he pulls it over his now bald and somewhat sickly-looking skull, has it adjusted by the coiffeur, who, while leaning over slightly, pulls and tugs at the hairpiece here and there and finally invites him with a hum to please have a look at himself over there, in that small adjacent room.

Hanging exactly opposite one another are two

floor-length mirrors framed in agate and carefully veiled in sheets of gauze because among certain rather old-fashioned Japanese there persists the superstition that there be a direct connection between one's reflection and the human soul. Nägeli positions himself between the looking glasses, and when his image multiplied by the hundred vanishes into infinitude, his eyelashes turn damp.

Can he perhaps sense that at exactly this moment his remarkably photogenic mother lies dying, his mother whose aristocratic neck never became wrinkled, she who for years wore a simple string of pearls over an ice-gray cashmere sweater and whose ash-colored hair, cut quite short between collarbone and jaw (as if a cold Alpine summer breeze had softly coiffed it forward at its brittle ends from behind), always outlined her face between her too-high cheekbones and her somewhat too-weak mouth and the sun-whitened spots between her hair and the skin of her temples—that while he is here in Japan she is dying, now, much too early, coughing?

The effect of the toupee in any case is altogether astonishing; at one stroke, the clock of his life has been set back by years. Delighted at the intimate, precarious pleasure of his foreign customer, the *sensei* (for that he is, a master of rejuvenation) asks him, with the raised tip of his forefinger to his lips, to take a seat in that swivel chair and now carefully pencils over the curvature of Nägeli's eyebrows, now dabs a brush into a jar filled with scarlet-red cream, and now with a steady hand paints the gentleman's cheeks in circular motions, while strokes of his knuckles expertly wipe away the excess color.

Now a rotation of the chair initiated by an invisible knee, which confuses him mildly, a new, scrutinizing look into the magic double mirror (while slightly sucking in his cheeks), a final snip with the little scissors— and an unruly eyebrow hair whose mission it has been for years to jut horizontally into space, groping just like an insect's antenna, vanishes without a trace. Payment for the procedure is rejected under vehement protests.

Outside the door to the establishment, Nägeli, full of disbelief at the markedly successful transformation of his appearance, gazes once more (not all too discreetly) at his reflection in the display window, turns himself around on the sidewalk in a hint of a pirouette and then, pioneer of metamorphosis, saunters down the street to the inviting scarlet rectangle of the *torii* of a nearby park or shrine. Happily striding through it, he walks awhile under a hyper-blue early summer sky, free from all thought, and then he pauses before an almost bare cherry tree, and he looks up into its pale-violet crown of blooms.

A mechanical bird made of artfully painted sheet metal sits there on a branch in the tree, cleaning its plumage and warbling: *fee-dee-bus*. A cherry blossom falls in death, dies in falling. It is perfect like this.

33.

Masahiko Amakasu and Ida von Üxküll are seated across from one another in the salon of the villa that has been rented by the Ministry for the foreign filmmakers. Legs crossed, they have between them on the low table a half-full bowl of snowily salted edamame and two rather questionable cocktails.

They smoke, tapping their ashes into a coconut shell on hand for this purpose, play with an automation dog whose spring seems to have a malfunction, leaf half-heartedly through fashion magazines. Shallow, soft jazz music, some popular song burbles out in the hall-way, or perhaps upstairs on the wooden gallery; it is not entirely apparent where the speakers are located. The servant was sent home around five.

Amakasu has screwed a monocle to his right eye; he

is wearing a tapered dark-blue woolen suit and a dark tie, the German woman, by contrast, that aviator's uniform that becomes her so well, jodhpurs, and tall boots. A few days ago she had the curls in her hair taken out and the result dyed platinum blond—not to better distinguish herself from Barbara Stanwyck, to whom she bears a strong resemblance, but rather simply to look even more German here in Japan.

With thumb and forefinger Ida tugs the cuffs of her blouse down the back of her hand as if trying to hide her wrists from the Japanese man—these she finds unattractive, even tomboyish. Her hands are not especially refined either, and at night she chews on her fingernails until the tips are exposed, ragged and bloody, which she attempts to conceal by day as best she can. Amakasu, who likewise chews on his fingernails, has developed the method of letting them grow out and then only biting them down to the point at which they exhibit the socially acceptable length.

Ida is expecting her fiancé, has been for days; he, the man who telegraphed his precise time of arrival from the steamship—can one really say this so harshly?— is quite the philistine, but she does feel some antsy anticipation nonetheless. Hopefully, she says, hopefully he's shaved his head by now.

He had always combed his hair over his pate from

the side, which she had never really noticed until one day, while vacationing together by the sea (they swam in what was for the end of June a still miserably cold Baltic), as Nägeli was ambushed from behind by a powerful wave, he had stumbled, minced about, and had forgotten to suck in his belly. Then, when he raised his arms in greeting, laughing and spewing fountains of salt water, she had seen the shoulder-length strand of hair hanging down from his temple, limp and dripping—except for this unsavory extension of hair and some tufts distributed here and there, he was almost entirely bald. He'd looked like a circus clown who'd gotten into a moronic accident and was now sadly hoping for applause, the poor thing.

Having said this to Amakasu, she leaves the humiliating topography of Nägeli's sexual character unmentioned, yet she sees before her eyes the tableau following their visit to the beach—abruptly fixed by a flash of memory, there, on the bed of an otherwise nondescript hotel room, a view onto the ocean—the spontaneous manifestation of which causes her to feel intensely embarrassed for Nägeli. He had penetrated her painfully, two drops of saliva, accompanied by a short and muffled sound of moaning, went splat on her back from his mouth, and after half a minute of miserable, pathetic sex, everything was already over.

But all men are vulnerable through their vanity and

so are controllable, Amakasu argues—it's quite simple: You simply have to twist it around such that *eikyō* develops, which unfortunately can only partly be translated by *influence*; these flaws, however, are the sole attributes that make the rather irrelevant male gender interesting in the first place, since you can get men to labor on your behalf. The less one as a woman has to do oneself, the better it is for the ostensible harmony between the sexes, he says, smiling, and then he stands up to fetch the two of them another drink, and in passing places his hand amicably on the young German woman's shoulder. A pleasant shudder passes through Ida.

Remembering that he has not eaten anything at all yesterday and today, Amakasu prepares a large piece of dark-brown pig liver in the kitchen. He unwraps it from the oily, opaque packing paper and lays it on the sideboard. He first takes a sharp kitchen knife from the drawer, but returns it as Westernized and imprecise after examining it, chooses a *tantō* from the shelf, and slices the raw meat into two equal halves, which flop away to the left and right of the knife with an obscene slump. Now he licks off the blade, almost sensually distorting his face. Sure, he cannot stand the sight of blood, but this delectable taste of iron! He rewraps the one piece, hastily wolfing down the other lobe of liver as though he were doing something illicit.

Ida lights a cigarette, decides against it, and pokes it into the sand-filled receptacle unsmoked. The cuckoo clock strikes quarter of; no bird appears squawking in the little wooden window.

34.

Now at long last: the sound of an approaching car, the slamming of doors, voices, footsteps on gravel, then the sound of the doorbell, once, twice, three times (as always three times, like before, in Switzerland), now the warm, muffled sound of a suitcase being dropped on the teak floor, the familiar *Ida!*, there it is, that pretentious, Swiss *I*, drawn out slightly in the back of the throat, my goodness, it's really him, she thinks, just now he'll come in and toss his hat on the sofa with a flick of the wrist.

In a fantastic mood, Emil Nägeli flings his hat onto the sofa as he walks in. Ida covers her mouth with her hand—her fiancé has grown ten years younger, his wrinkles have been magically erased (Amakasu calls out from the kitchen, unfortunately they're out of vodka, can't they also make martinis with *shōchū*?).

Goodness, there's a dark-brown hairpiece stuck to Nägeli's head, he's already bending over to kiss Ida. The tweed fabric of his sleeve grazes her cheek, as always he smells of pencil shavings, she cups his neck with outstretched hands (since, as she realizes with a tingle, she does still love him a little), he wrests himself from her, throws himself backward onto the sofa, and deftly slips off the brown wingtips (wasn't he supposed to have removed them at the door?), which vanish beneath the coffee table, one after the other, as if they had a life of their own.

Did she miss him terribly all these months, yes, and besides, what sort of ghastly house had they put her up in anyhow; its (he searches for the right word, shaking his head) eclectic style, which just doesn't seem to fit at all into this elegant, sedately green street in Akasaka District, might best be described as *Tudorbethan*. He smirks at the heavy, medieval-looking furniture, at the phony coat of arms, look, there are even stag antlers hanging on the wall next to the dark-wood fireplace; beside that are neo-Gothic chairs whose seats are upholstered one and all in various Scottish tartans, it's all a little bit gaudy, one does feel like one's on a film set in this house, but wait, he's got something for his darling, he's really so very happy and so on and so forth.

Over and over Ida begins to ask him why he looks

so much younger, why he's now wearing a toupee, if that's perhaps powder and makeup or whether he's had an operation to make his face look more pleasing, that's the sort of thing, she wants to say, she's learned film actresses do—for example, having their molars removed in order to seem ageless—but he doesn't let her get a word in edgewise, as if he has to make up for their lost time together in fast-motion; he chatters ceaselessly, recounting the ship's passage, how this glorious country has stirred him, the impressive train ride past Fujiyama, and his decision to wear a wig from now on. No, no, he's been made up only very lightly by the hairdresser. Oh, Ida! What about you?

No matter, he is already hurrying back to the foyer without waiting for an answer (he almost—*sumimasen deshita!*—collides with Amakasu, who instantly and with a steady hand raises up the tray with the three drinks) to open his suitcase and retrieve the promised gift; it is a book about Noh theater, by Ezra Pound, inscribed to Ida.

Ida had thought the volume lost; it was given to her ten years ago when she was a very young, impressionable girl of not quite seventeen and misplaced straightaway at an outing in Ticino at which she drank more Champagne than she had planned.

He has found the book, really and truly: *pour*

Ida—ma Iseult assoiffée, il faudrait bien l'arroser; thus reads the dedication by Pound in his spidery hand on the first page, *merci vielmal*, Emil, thank you so much, wherever did you *find* this?

And *this*, by the way, is Mr. Amakasu, she says, as the book is tossed onto a side table and immediately forgotten—her teenage infatuation with Ezra Pound is embarrassing to her in front of this Japanese man with whom she has enjoyed sexual intercourse today three times already and most abundantly yesterday and the entire week before.

Just now in the foyer Amakasu and Nägeli have sniffed each other out in a dream anamnestically, so to speak, and assured themselves of the other's true being. Ordinarily this is done by people of their kind in fractions of seconds, and they ignore each other from then on; the path from rebirth to rebirth is much too arduous and cruel to have to share it with other initiates. The dead are profoundly lonesome creatures, there is no solidarity among them, they are all born alone, die, and are reborn alone as well.

Amakasu has evidently been primed for Nägeli's anticipated arrival by a letter from Hugenberg; that the man belongs to the same species as he, moreover, makes the matter no less interesting, even though the Swiss film director seems not to harbor the slightest suspicion about Masahiko's relationship with Ida. Amakasu has not the faintest idea where this will lead him, but does have the impression that it will be a place both wonderful and strange, and while reentering the salon, he experiences a trick of the senses that allows him for a few seconds to catch the malty primordial scent of the sea.

35.

Nägeli can safely unpack his things later, just this once he oughtn't be so small-minded, Ida would so very much like to go to the cinema, wasn't that a fabulous idea? Afterward they could grab a small bite to eat, sometimes she craves something simple like a plain lettuce salad, the entire cuisine here, with the exception of the fried pork schnitzel and the omelets, is just too kooky for her. Emil will soon see (as if he hadn't long since intuited it himself on his journey) how things are done here in Japan, the magic suffusing ordinary things, one can really only get to know a country best at the movies, please, he should just say yes already.

In the cinema then, as the theater lights dim, Nägeli's hand reaches for Ida's knee, and while the tip of his hastily lit cigarette glows orange-red in the white light of the projector, the hat in his lap conceals his frighteningly pitiful erection.

Masahiko declares that the famous director, Yasujirō Ozu, operating quite like he, Nägeli, did in *Die Windmühle*, had the lips of the actress Mitsuko Yoshikawa expressly painted as snow-white as her whole visage, highlighting only the middle of her lower lip with a bloodred dot, as if one were dealing here with a bird of death. Her dark eyes appear to the Swiss director as devoid of life as the rubbery texture of her chalky complexion.

She's filmed slightly from below, just look, Amakasu says, the camera is kept at a height relative to the tatami mat. This is because there aren't any chairs and beds in the Japanese sense of space; the usual higher-angle perspective of camera and observer is an exclusively Western way of seeing.

While other patrons of the cinema a few rows back hiss indignantly that those down front ought to please keep quiet and not cause such disturbances, Amakasu continues that, luckily, Ozu steadfastly refuses to accept sound film, that mendacious, imperialist, Western notion, and besides, disallowing dialogue is also absolutely applicable to Japanese society. One doesn't discuss things; that's just barbaric.

Nägeli begins to tune him out, leans back, cocks his head a bit as he always does in the presence of genius, and is secretly and in his Protestant manner delighted that Amakasu knows *Die Windmühle*.

There is a honking outside the cinema, a siren sounds and drifts away again, and in the off-glow of the film being projected onto the screen in front of them, Nägeli wonders whether Mr. Amakasu, at whose face, by turns brightly and somberly lit, he is staring incessantly from the side—goodness, he cannot escape his charisma; there is something about the man that unsettles him deep within—whether, uh, yes, that's right, whether Amakasu himself shouldn't simply play the leading role in his new film.

The picture is over, and the three retreat from the theater into the foyer amid the disapproving looks of the other cinemagoers, and Amakasu ignores the naked young red-painted woman in the farthest corner of the cinema signaling to him with her protruding tongue. Nägeli orders three glasses of sparkling wine and, after a bit of throat-clearing and foot-shuffling, asks whether the two would like to star in his film as principal actors.

He's planning to make a film, and that's why he's in Japan. Amakasu does not mention that he himself invited him via Hugenberg; he had not exactly hoped it would be *this* guileless child, but there you are.

Nägeli, in any case, has thought it over long and carefully, he wants to work without a script, which indeed has never been done before, but he imagines it more or less like just taking the camera along everywhere, it'll be a simple handheld camera, he'd shoot in natural light and follow the two of them, Masahiko and Ida, on their journeys through the city, into the streetcar, into restaurants and cafés, into museums, hotels, everywhere. Sure, right now none of this has been fully thought out yet, but one's got to start somewhere, and so why not now, and what do they think?

He'd need to go hiking for a few days in the hills beforehand to concentrate, go walking a bit by himself, then he'd return to Tokyo, and then they could get started.

36.

Back at their villa, Nägeli prepares the two Swiss 16mm
Bolex film cameras, as well as the Bell & Howell de-
vice UFA had flown separately to him in Tokyo. The
clasp on the housing is a bit jammed, but after a little
squeezing, the cameras are loaded with their film cartridges. He cleans them with a dustcloth and first
chats about how agreeable and highly intelligent this
Japanese man is, even his command of German is quite
outstanding, and then he relates that he's now finally
free after his father's death, that his spirit and his art
will no longer be encumbered by anything. His insufferable state of apathy has been overcome, Ida can't
imagine what a burden he's cast off, that's also probably why, he lies, he seems to look so much younger.

Ida yawns like a lioness, complains of a migraine,
and disappears for over an hour into the bathroom.
When she has finished her evening toilette, Nägeli is
lying back on the bed in strap garters, snoring, like a
sluggish, blond reptile. The toupee lies beside him on the

pillow, which has been faintly stained with makeup. She picks up the hairy thing and lets it slide through her fingers, shuddering imperceptibly; she gently lays it back, creeps through the bedroom down the steps to the salon, smokes several cigarettes on the sofa downstairs, empties a glass of flat Champagne, draws her knees to her chest, and yearns for Amakasu's skillful, tender hands. If it weren't so sad with Emil, she thinks, it would all be so very amusing.

On the way back into the bedroom, she inadvertently rams her foot against the head of the suction spout jutting from the wall at ankle height and thereby activates the house's central vacuum system, whose nerve-racking mechanical whooshing, welling forth from the bowels of the home, combined with the sounds of Nägeli's fluttering snores, cheats her—it is almost insufferable—of two whole further hours of sleep.

Having finally nodded off in the early morning, and after wandering down a long street wreathed in flowers, at the abrupt end of which she pulls open a heavy, chiseled wooden door with some difficulty, she somewhat timidly enters the realm of the dead for a very short while, that world-in-between where dream, film, and memory haunt one another, and there she hears a disembodied aspiration; it sounds to her like a sustained *hah*.

37.

The next day they drive out together in a convertible to the city's edge, to Asaka's new golf course. Nägeli brings along his handheld cameras. He spent the previous night, which was overshadowed by a profound feeling of embarrassment, unsuccessfully groping about on Ida.

Translating, Amakasu reads aloud to them from the newspapers briskly rustling in the wind. They report that the seven young naval officers who had killed the prime minister had, all of them, surrendered to the authorities after it had become clear to them that their coup attempt had failed. To be sure, they had been tried right away, but waves of indignation had sloshed up throughout the whole country, and yesterday, when a delegation had cut off their pinky fingers and sent them to the government as a sign of their obsequious deference, the young people were hastily and unexpectedly acquitted. Chaplin had gone into hiding somewhere, heavily armed.

Nägeli, having risen from the backseat of the car,

Bolex in hand, films Ida at the wheel of the cabriolet and Masahiko reading from the newspaper, and he pans the camera back and forth between the two, discovering in the viewfinder (as if he were unable to see it in real life) the stain of intimacy between his fiancée and his Japanese host.

Look, the way he lights her cigarette with a smile, how obvious it is. And now they are standing on the saturated green of the golf course, and Amakasu shows her the correct swing, knees bent slightly (Nägeli is still at it, filming, tossing the full cartridges into the cloth bag he has brought along), the iron raised to the right, the sky segmented by pretty clouds; he is standing behind her, thus, in a loose embrace, guiding her hands around the grip of the club.

All this cannot possibly be happening, Nägeli thinks, dissembling, lowering the camera, smiling, nodding, waving, biting at a thumbnail whose crescent edge just will not come off, damn it.

A wind whips up, and the three sit on the camel hair blanket, eating the ham sandwiches they packed, their paper wrappings tumbling over the golf course. Masahiko, in high spirits now, poking them both in the sides, amused, slaps his forehead with his palm and runs over to the parking lot to fetch the forgotten bottle of Champagne from the car.

Nägeli looks at Ida, reaches tenderly, almost shyly for her hand, his eyebrows raised in a feeble query, as if they could resolve right here and now between them what is still, however, in the realm of conjecture; a fathomless, yellow, trembling feeling of powerlessness has taken control of him, he who has always derided jealousy as an emotion of the bourgeoisie and who nevertheless has refused to perceive Ida as a subject in her own right, separate from him. She withdraws her hand as Amakasu trots up again. Nägeli looks at his own, which is quite moist and rubbery inside.

38.

The following day Nägeli is sitting in the living room of the ministerial rental villa, wringing his hands, sucking on one of his fingertips. He gets up to fetch a glass from the oaken cabinet and discovers that there is a small hatchway concealed in the cupboard, right there on the inner back panel.

He looks around sheepishly, no one's there (where have those two run off now?), wedges his way into the cabinet, opens the latch, and climbs through into the bowels of the house, noticing in passing that here within the wooden structure it smells as it did in those intolerable farmhouse parlors of his youth, like dust and something greasy.

He feels as though he were suddenly behind or, rather, *inside* the sets of a theater. The crossbeams and braces in here are joined to one another without nails, and while realizing from this perspective that the entire house has, distastefully, merely feigned a Western ambience, he ascends the bottommost rung of a stepladder leaning there, at the top of which a bright beam of light is shining through a hole onto the opposite wall.

He climbs all the way up and spies through the peephole into the bedroom; a painting on the wall there is daubed with the red splotches of a modern artist. Trembling, he observes the monstrous phantasm of Masahiko and Ida, writhing about naked on the bed, and he sees, over and over and over again, how Masahiko, amid her submissive cries muffled by the strip of white linen plugging her mouth, finally mounts her. Her right thigh and the top of her freckled shoulders have been bruised by the pressure of his fingers on her skin.

The disgusting effrontery of their moaning together, the humiliation of the beholder. The pale-blue iris of his eye at the hole, illuminated by the scene in the room, almost as if his gaze itself were the projector of this abomination. Nägeli swallows three times, it is as if he had molasses in his mouth, as if his diaphragm were melting.

He swiftly descends the ladder, searches for and finds the exit, climbs out of the cabinet, and in anguish grabs the Bolex that has been quietly waiting for this moment on a side table. Now, quickly back into the innards of the house, up to the peephole, where the lens of the camera is inserted, the whole thing soundproofed with the sleeve of his sweater so that no whirring sound makes it through to the bedroom. He pulls the shutter release and waits until the film cartridge is filled with this crude mélange of slapstick and tragedy, infinitely thankful there is no soundtrack that could play back Masahiko's and Ida's cries.

Back in the parlor Nägeli tears the wig from his head in disgust and throws it into the kitchen rubbish, wipes the vestiges of makeup from his face at the sink, sees the sharp *tantō* lying there, and briefly considers ramming it into his throat or else running upstairs into the bedroom to instigate a bloodbath.

Nonsense, he thinks, wondering how he might contact Chaplin, ask him for his revolver, friendly-like, among filmmakers. Damn it, that'll get him nowhere,

they are all in league with one another—Ida has probably already slept with *him* as well. These harrowing
visions martyr what were raw nerves to begin with,
which feel like they have been dipped in an acid bath.

39.

He packs his suitcase and a duffel bag with the cameras and film cartridges, curses Masahiko and Ida,
wishing that they should please die swiftly and painfully, gives a floor lamp a forceful but unimaginative
kick, and hurriedly quits the villa.

He rushes to the nearest train station and in the
subsequent weeks travels aimlessly around the Empire, into the warm south, to Nagasaki and Fukuoka,
then back again, far northeastward toward Tokyo, to
Kanagawa Prefecture. He's left his hat at the villa—
oh God, if that isn't symbolic.

Deranged and befuddled, he sleeps for but a few
hours in lowly flophouses, shooting some cartridges of
a film that is meaningless to him; pilgrims heading out

for this or that shrine, automobile accidents, lonesome country train stations illuminated at night, stooped old women helping with the rice harvest, bamboo groves waving in the wind, a paper cup heedlessly discarded and trampled flat. He eats almost nothing anymore, does not bathe, no longer brushes his teeth.

One evening he is seated before a bowl of noodle soup gone cold, in a city whose name he has forgotten. An orange-red paper lantern covers the lightbulb at the door, next to which is leaned an old bicycle. The worried innkeeper serves the unkempt foreigner a large glass of tea, unsure whether she should not instead fetch the police; then she realizes that living directly beside her humble tavern is a man of letters who might understand the stranger's language.

She wipes her hands on her apron and walks next door to call upon the man who, grown curious at her description, allows her to lead him to Nägeli's table and addresses him politely in English: Is everything all right, pardon me, the gentleman looks so desolate, couldn't he perhaps help him, without of course wanting to offend?

Nägeli glances up, swallows, and two tender tears trickle down his cheeks; the innkeeper looks at the ground, mortified at this open display of emotion, and the writer, who is a good-natured person, takes a seat at the table, removes his spectacles, and asks the woman for some rice wine and two glasses.

And Nägeli, touched, invents some story about being a tourist whose wife left him in Tokyo or the like; by no stretch of the imagination can he, in this bleak place, tell the truth, which is that he is a has-been director who once made *one* good film many years ago and then, after his artistic bankruptcy and his father's death, in a whiff of greed and hubris, let that German monster Hugenberg shuffle him to Japan to realize a project here that was whispered into his ear one drunken Berlin night by two film critics—it would all seem too outrageous (that in reality Amakasu himself invited him he suspects not at all).

The writer takes the director, along with his baggage, over to his house, where a carelessly framed reproduction of Guido Reni's *Saint Sebastian* hangs next to the kitchen entrance, and he orders him first into the bathroom. And all at once, after he has looked in the mirror and is shocked at his reflection—his buzzed hair has grown back only in patches—Nägeli, overcome with emotion, is on the brink of relating the unconscionable events that have befallen him.

After washing his face and rinsing out his mouth,

he returns to the kitchen, takes a seat, and bites into the rice cake so amicably offered to him, and he runs his hands through the damp tufts of hair. There's the smell of Pears soap. It's very possible that he's begun to cry again.

Stop, he is told, he must now get a hold of himself, please, the writer would very much like to massage him first, and anyway, it really just comes down to this: that there are only two great principles in the world closely related to one another, sexuality and suicide. Both topoi, as he calls them, are permeated by transcendence and mutual interference, and Nägeli, whose shoulders the man behind him now seizes and kneads fiercely, wonders how he might escape here unscathed.

It's very likely, says the author, as Nägeli slides back and forth on his chair, that the great rustling beyond God can be experienced only by the one who's resolved himself to suicide, with concentrated, irrefutable, manly virility.

Nägeli, who only now notices the many knives in the kitchen, forgets the tears circumnavigating his unshaven chin only moments ago and looks back with a stern Swiss glare at the man, who throws up both hands defensively, as if he hadn't meant it that way at all.

With clenched fists and the chorale of his singing

blood in his ears, Nägeli rises from the chair, brusquely shoves the man out of his way, grabs his luggage idling by the entrance, and pushes open the unlocked sliding door to the street with a violent gesture: out, away from this place.

PART THREE

40.

Charles Chaplin deposits the white dimpled golf ball
stamped with *Veritas* onto the spot in front of him
marked with green chalk. The sky is cloudless, the Pacific conducts itself pacifically. The steamer's screws
twirl through the ocean in a monotone, as whisks would
in an aquarium.

Chaplin raises the flashing golf club behind his head.
And no sooner has the iron swung in an immaculate
silvery arc past his two-tone shoes than the ball hurtles
aloft into the azure, projectile-like, only to splash down
again finally, inaudible, invisible, and of no consequence,
far out into the ocean. *Ver-i-tas*, Chaplin whistles to dis-
guise his rage.

They have made a hasty departure from Tokyo, said
no farewells, just tossed the barest necessities of cloth-
ing into a few suitcases and made for Yokohama, to the
harbor, under the cover of night. Amakasu had asked
Ida at the pier if she really did want to come along, for
there'd be no turning back later of course, and she'd

smiled at him—*in love* is putting it too strongly, but then again maybe not. A deafening and melancholy blow of the steamship's horn marked its departure.

Amakasu, who has removed his white blazer and rolled up the cuffs of his dress shirt, lights a cigarette, wiping his lower lip with his thumb. When the next golf ball vanishes toward the horizon, he squints so as to better follow the parabola of the falling rubber star. Not wanting to accept Chaplin's once more aggressively proffered golf club, he buries his hands in his pockets; his lack of athleticism borders on the pathological. Chaplin winds up and swings.

The sorts of things people think up to pass the time on a sea voyage like this. One can borrow tennis rackets from the captain, play shuffleboard, Ping-Pong, billiards, even various footballs and rugby balls in all shapes and sizes are available for the passengers—to do so one must sign up on a list displayed prominently at the staircase to the salon.

And every other evening there is a film screening, mostly, if the sea is calm, on the screen erected for this purpose on the quarterdeck of the *Tatsuta Maru*, bound for Los Angeles.

Thus, of an evening, Chaplin, Ida, and Masahiko lounge about on the pretty striped deck chairs and probably watch every film shown on the sea crossing.

All the while they drink large quantities of Brandy Alexander and many a cup of the free coffee on offer. They watch Karl Freund's *The Mummy*, both ghostly and amusing, and Leni Riefenstahl's *The Blue Light*, Murnau's *Tabu* and *Frankenstein* with Boris Karloff, and an old film with Harold Lloyd is screened, too, which Chaplin, visibly rattled, shrugs off as uninspired; oh, he says, that's just *amateurish kinetics*.

Kono spends the entire voyage to Los Angeles sulking in his third-class cabin after Chaplin brusquely informs him at embarkation, after he is yet again about to puff himself up, that Kono should just keep his mouth shut for once, otherwise he'll be fired, and he shouldn't get the idea that Chaplin is an idiot and hasn't noticed that he's been stealing middling sums from him for years; *that* he can still stomach, but to have not only subjected him to this nation of insane people, but also hoodwinked him into an assassination attempt on his life? That's just nefarious, and it borders on psychosis. Oh, come to think of it, he is simply sacked, right now, *finito*.

At night—Masahiko has already fallen asleep next to her—Ida wakes up, leaves their shared cabin, proceeds barefoot to the quarterdeck, touches the railing, and stares up into the overpowering, random pattern of the nocturnal sky.

Chaplin has prophesied to her, while drinking large numbers of cocktails, that her glorious triumph in American cinema, which he would like to launch for her, will immediately be without equal—to which she replies with somewhat put-on coyness that she unfortunately won't be able to get rid of ze German accent so easily; but, but, that very thing is terrifically well received right now, she should just dive right into sound film, and anyway, her white-blonde hair and her freckles (and of course her great talent, too) guarantee quite a career, it often happens very fast, naturally he knows the right people and will introduce her to them all, he's already got a few in mind. The whole time he charms her and flops around like an eel, but why should he say such things if there isn't anything to them?

Ida wishes fervently to see a shooting star burn up in the night sky over the Pacific—then she might have another wish—but the black firmament above remains uncrossed by comets; the stars flicker with inexorable indifference. By day innumerable golf balls are catapulted into the sea again, and during mealtimes a certain apathy surfaces, an odd flatness.

One evening—they have been drinking more than usual and watching Howard Hawks's *Scarface* together on the ship's screen, which snaps in the wind—a nasty fight breaks out between Chaplin and Amakasu.

Japan has been completely and utterly spoiled for the actor—he puts it like that, too—and then he swiftly becomes abusive and insulting as well. Enraged, he shouts that a peaceful, pan-Asian socialism under Japan's guidance has no chance, if for no other reason than the Japanese are, quite simply, fascists; as a nation they obviously take pleasure in debasing and humiliating others. They presume that everyone around them is a barbarian—the whole globe, that's how they see it, is populated with base, effeminate, and above all cultureless serfs.

Ida heads off to bed, saying she wants nothing to do with this nonsense. Amakasu smiles a hint too smugly and likewise intends to take his leave, whereupon Chaplin grabs him by the sleeve and ushers him behind the screen, out of earshot, the whole while insisting how happy he is now to be returning to a free country, Amakasu will soon see how accommodating they are in America, the individual is in demand there, the individual bears responsibility, not the collective. And he empties his glass in one gulp.

Amakasu waves it off condescendingly, the recent unspeakable press conference still in mind. He's thankful that Chaplin and he will experience this sea voyage together, but not so blindly thankful that he need listen to such naïve commonplaces from a man who obviously lacks any political understanding whatsoever. Chaplin ought to rejoice in his magnificent film successes, in earning recognition and acclaim the whole world over. Or does he perhaps worry that he'll miss the boat with sound film? For it'll come, guaranteed, indeed it's already here, except in Japan. But that is somewhere he never wants to go back to, he adds as a little dig.

Aha, so I'm a little prole, eh? Chaplin says, and Amakasu replies that he never said that (can he perhaps read minds?). And then suddenly Chaplin draws his revolver from the waistband of his suit trousers, holds the barrel against the other's stomach, tottering, and commands Amakasu to jump into the ocean or he'll pull the trigger.

Amakasu is aghast. Wait, just a minute. He can't possibly be serious? Oh, he is, oh so very serious. It's like this: Chaplin hates his guts, he always has, since that reception at the American legation. The Jap can choose freely: a hole in his innards or the minuscule chance of survival at swim in the Pacific. Hawaii isn't quite sixty miles north, so take your pick.

Amakasu considers whether he might be fast enough to grab the gun; Chaplin is visibly plastered, maybe he's not capable of pulling the trigger so quickly; could also be that the pistol is not even loaded. In fractions of a second the limited options and their consequences race through his head, but it always ends with unimaginable pain in the pit of his stomach.

He climbs the railing, carefully swinging one leg over to the seaward side. Chaplin staggers toward him and shoves him over into the ocean. Then he tosses the revolver in after him.

Later he will tell Ida he didn't see Amakasu, he, Chaplin, also went to bed—for God's sake, the poor man didn't perhaps tumble overboard at night drunk, did he? He says the same thing to the captain. He is the most famous actor in the world; people have always believed everything he says.

41.

Masahiko splutters, swimming a few strokes in whichever direction. Immediately sober, he sees the lights of the steamer growing smaller and smaller, and as he swallows a few mouthfuls of salt water, he becomes aware of the whole horrible enormity of his situation.

If only he had something to hold on to, a piece of wood, it didn't matter what. If only he knew what direction Hawaii was. If only he'd let himself be shot in the gut.

He floats on his back and drifts up and down the wave troughs. The moon illuminates the dreadful scene, glassy and gray. The water is not especially cold. If the sea current were impelling him forward with a speed of perhaps four miles per hour, he would be in Hawaii in a good eighteen hours, provided, of course, that the current is moving him that way in the first place. This is it. Numbly he maps the position of the islands in the ocean, there are around eight, that much he knows; he imagines them to be like a rake in whose distantly placed prongs he will be caught. He has thirty hours left, but if by that point he has not reached land, he will die of thirst. If only he hadn't drunk so many cocktails— Chaplin, that fucking lunatic.

From wave to wave he keeps drifting off to sleep for a few seconds. The whole matter has something tremendously clear about it, and ridiculous, too; he doesn't want to die, nor is he *not* dead. He hears a crackling and crinkling underwater at ear level; it is the primal sound of this planet, in the middle of which he perceives, a long way off, a submerged, oscillating noise—it is the skittish, modulated squeaking of sea mammals singing to one another in the ocean over vast stretches of loneliness.

Nothing is without meaning, he thinks, and he imagines himself finally rinsed onto a beach by waves that foam over him, breaking with gentle and feeble softness; there on the shore he sees crabs and shells and rocks, the tangible, perceptible bleached skeleton of the earth, and above, stretching in breathless blue, the infinite gift of the heavens.

42.

After arriving by rail in northern Hokkaidō, Nägeli crosses over on a ferry to the Kuril Islands, that archipelago on the way to Siberia. At the harbor he walks up to a fishing boat, gesturing somewhat helplessly, bowing, pointing to the northeastern horizon. The shrimp fishermen take him along a ways, to the next island, and the following one, and he considers giving them the bag with the cameras in gratitude after filming their rugged, kind faces and their nets, but he thinks the better of it: could be that he may need the devices yet.

At the border to Russia, the fishing boat is stopped by grim-looking Soviet naval troops; they set over in a dinghy and inspect the crew, while a heavy machine gun on the coast guard ship is trained on them. Nägeli babbles that he doesn't exactly have a visa, but he's a Swiss naturalist; might he at least ride along until just off Kamchatka? The Soviet officer on duty of course does not allow him to continue his journey and begins examining the sack with the cameras.

Before he ends up in any further predicaments, Nägeli gives away all his cigarettes to the soldiers, hands the officer his remaining dollars, the fishermen and Nägeli bow, and amid thousands of apologies, the Japanese do an about-face and deposit him back on the coast of Hokkaidō. Leaving, they call out to him a friendly warning about brown bears that will sometimes attack humans this time of year.

He crisscrosses wild Hokkaidō, where now, in the early Japanese summer, the slopes and coastal cliffs are engirdled by the violet blossoms of wild lilies and primroses. Nägeli wanders with neither route nor plan, farther and farther, constructs shelters for himself each evening from branches and twigs or sleeps under the stars, fills his water bottle in the brooks, catches fish with his bare hands and eats them raw, and attempts, treading cautiously, to film the brown bears that do show up now and again.

Nature seems to him impetuous and lush and full of power, and at night he dreams of vast extinct volcanoes whose slopes appear all a-jumble in the distance. Many a time does he in fact see their orange, calming glow in the night sky, hundreds of miles away. A family of foxes follows him for several days at a safe remove; nesting birds tweet *fee-dee-bus* at their brethren moving westward in the sky.

Several times while walking, he senses a small hand reaching for his own, feels his thumb being enclosed by a child's hand; if he looks, there is naturally no one there, but if he hikes farther, then he cannot shake the very concrete sensation that someone small is walking with and beside him; his instinct tells him he is being watched, but whenever he turns around, he is utterly alone.

He is certain these peculiar feelings owe to the solitude of nature, and he concerns himself no further with them. Yet, suddenly, his father is back, after long weeks and months; there is his suntanned, carefully shaved neck with the ice-gray, half-millimeter-long stubble, the cheerful age spots, the twinkle in his eye, yes now, damn it, his father did have a sense of humor beneath all that recursive, elegant brutality.

And all at once he is sure that his father simply stopped liking him one day because he, Emil, had at some point withdrawn his hand, because for an older child, so he had thought, it was no longer appropriate to walk holding one's father's hand. Yes, he thinks, that had been the break between the two of them, and it was all his fault and not that of his father, whom he suddenly misses very much.

<h2 style="text-align:center">43.</h2>

After a week's foot march, during which Nägeli acquires thoroughly tormenting blisters, when he reaches the impoverished, almost deserted little town of Asahikawa, shielded and overtopped by long-extinct volcanoes (as if he had always carried these perfect mountains, siblings of Fujiyama, in his brain's repertoire of images), he walks for a spell down the main street, lined left and right with slapdash timbered wooden houses, in search of an inn or a hotel.

Instead, he comes upon a shop, probably a general store, a souvenir shop, and he steps through the door of wood and glass. A little bell jingles above him in the quiet of the afternoon. Although he first clears his throat loudly and then calls out a hello, no one appears. The shop seems abandoned, maybe even derelict.

Once his eyes have adjusted to the cushioned murk, he sees light-brown dust everywhere; lying spread out on tables are curtains of dark-red velvet woven with golden silk threads, sitting on top of them, in turn, are stuffed owls and kingfishers, scattered beside them silver forks removed from sets of cutlery, there is a dainty tea service, dried flowers, a dented yet still discernibly finely wrought samovar, there, a rusted toy train, light-wooden shoe trees inside buckskin ankle boots, a reproduction of Voltaire's death mask.

Several paintings hang over the radiator, which, upon closer inspection, turn out to be quite exquisite. Here, at the edge of Asia, he feels as though he were inside a memory chamber of an old, lost, long-forgotten Europe. Nägeli flips the light switch on the wall beside him, retrieves his Bolex camera, and films the room and everything in it with a slow, steady hand.

44.

The first few days in Los Angeles are so terrifically exciting! Radiated from above and lulled by the Mediterranean-mild Californian light—which only the envious could consider mediocre—Ida crisscrosses the megalopolis by streetcar, stopping now here to eat a hot dog, now there to pet a little dachshund in MacArthur Park. She attends endless cocktail receptions and visits the numerous museums to admire the American paintings exhibited in them, which in their shocking, naïve vitality oppose traditional European modernisms; she feels as if she were mixed up in a glorious whirlwind blowing her here and there through a city with diversions and a richness of culture far superior to those in Europe.

First and foremost Ida is to act in a film with which UFA hopes to introduce the United States to Heinz Rühmann, who is completely unknown in this country, but he declines Ida as his partner because he, for his part, does not wish to act with someone unknown. He of course can no longer recall the evening spent with Nägeli in Berlin and does not even make the connection between Ida and the Swiss director to begin with. The film does not materialize, and Rühmann will never travel to the States.

While auditioning for the next project she is told, okay, her aviator look may have been passé for years now, but she can have the role. Seems she had a powerful advocate, wink, wink. Admittedly, it is only a B-picture with Wallace Beery, but she throws herself with élan and zeal into the role of a housewife who sticks with her wrestler husband even though he suffers one ringing defeat after another. She firmly believes in him and emboldens him, but after his victory in the big, all-decisive match in Chicago, he cheats on her with a whore.

The script is dreadfully written, and the bloated, doughy Beery pinches her behind incessantly during the shoot and painfully squeezes her breasts when they are alone together one day in the dressing trailer, but she is not to be deterred, she wants to become a star, and this is ultimately part of it.

Alas, because a contract between Paramount Pictures and Metro-Goldwyn-Mayer comes into force, the final cut of the film *Spirit of the Fight* is shelved, and it disappears in an archive, never to be released. Ida receives a small cancellation fee and the prospect of acting in a Western in the foreseeable future, provided she loses thirty pounds.

After she has nearly starved herself to death for a month, the studio lets it be known that, thanks, but she has little discernible talent for acting, which might not be all that important, but unfortunately the hot-blooded South American type is in demand now, and the cool Nordic woman she embodies is outmoded. There might still be the possibility of plastic surgery if she were willing to do it. No, she is not. Well, they tell her, then unfortunately the studio's hands are tied. One more suggestion for the future: she really ought to change her name; not a soul here can pronounce it.

She thus begins cleaning, first on the side, then all day long, for a very well-known actress. She has been informed that the lady doesn't want to hire any blacks or any Jews, and that's why she, Aryan that she is, may start immediately; for the time being she needs to buy a pale-blue housemaid's uniform and report every morning to Sunset Boulevard in Beverly Hills, at the gate of an imposing villa, shaded by tall palm trees and built in the Spanish Mission style.

Each day in the late morning, the actress appears on the gallery of the house, her face slathered in moisturizing cream, wearing her dressing gown and accompanied by her two German mastiffs, Arthur and Lancelot. She behaves insufferably, drops her cigarette ashes wherever she likes, throws slices of salami and entire Qing vases at the staff when she is hungover, and on afternoons lies by the swimming pool naked and oiled up and in sunglasses, the riding crop in her idly outstretched hand, two cucumber slices on her eyes.

She seems only to be lying in wait for Ida to make some sort of mistake. A large dinner is planned during which Ida is to assist in serving soup and such things. When company arrives and steps up to the festively bedecked table after having sipped aperitifs in the yellow salon, she sees through a gap in the door to the kitchen that Charlie Chaplin is standing among the guests, tanned brown and in the best of humors. She bursts out to embrace him, a girl somewhat past her prime, emaciated and white-aproned, as if she were an addled fan; with an embarrassed grin Chaplin turns to the hostess, who then dresses Ida down and orders her out, back into the kitchen, where she cuffs her something powerful, once on the left and once on the right, and fires her on the spot.

45.

After a long voyage back to Switzerland, Nägeli enters his little flat in Zurich-Niederdorf, makes himself a cup of tea, skims the considerable stack of mail that has accumulated on his kitchen table, lights three cigarettes in a row, and while smoking feeds into his projector the film he has provisionally edited on the brand-new Steenbeck machine over at Nordisk in Oerlikon. After watching it twice, he smiles to himself silently and with pleasure because he sees it is a masterpiece.

He locks the apartment door from the outside, strolls down to the Limmat, which flows, sedate and placid, out of the lake, and for a long while observes the swans as they slip their heads with grace—it is now late autumn—under their wings. In the shallow, transparently shimmering waters of the riverbank, he discovers the slowly rotating spokes of a bicycle. In the distance beyond the lake, to the southeast, the snowcapped Alps are visible, and high above them, towering up in the föhn wind, there are the clouds he would stare at for hours when he was a child.

His hair is now the usual length again, he feels it in the brisk wind, touching his scalp with a shrug to see how the bald spot there on the back of his head has spread. From the long walk in Hokkaidō he has grown muscular and slim; there is something remote about his gaze, almost dreamlike.

Switzerland is no longer quite as strange to him as it was even a year ago. Apparently he has been missed, for in the intervening period there have been second thoughts about his creative work, and he has been both offered a guest professorship in Bern and awarded some sort of bronze medal in Romandy. What's more, he has been asked to give a series of lectures at the University of Zurich on the future of Swiss cinema, and he catches himself delighting in these new, bourgeois, even almost friendly affectations of his homeland.

He shows a rough cut of his film, which he has titled like this book, in a small, unimposing screening room in the Seefeld district, quite near the opera house. It is so very warm on this late afternoon; lightning sizzles from the clouds over the lake.

A female pianist and an unfortunately rather ungifted cellist accompany the black-and-white, silently flickering scenes; a Japanese man and a light-blonde young woman can be seen, he reading the newspaper in an open-top car; then a golf ball receding up elliptically into the heavens; the snowy cone of an extinct volcano; a dark junk room filled with worthless old trinkets; jittery, blurry animals that look like brown bears; close-ups of the rugged hands of Asian sailors mending their nets; the long-take shot of a trampled paper cup. Not all viewers stay awake.

Afterward there is restrained applause and four chilled bottles of Valais Fendant. A couple of receptive journalists have come, as have a few friends. The next day, they show Nägeli the newspapers amid approving laughter; in them he is declared an avant-garde and a surrealist—in the *Neue Zürcher Zeitung*, however, mentally deficient. *And this in Switzerland!* it says there. The passages of the film in which Amakasu and Ida have sexual intercourse with one another are addressed only to the extent that one writes what a good example they are for those tawdry and scheming tendencies in art that meanwhile, alas, are taking hold everywhere. In Germany, Hugenberg has been relieved by Joseph Goebbels, who seems to have forgotten, or has repressed, that Nägeli will forever owe UFA one film.

Sometimes, although not often, Nägeli thinks of Ida and Masahiko. He has heard through friends of friends that both have gone to America and been married there. She's probably become an actress and has come into good circumstances. That cultureless land does little for him. Hate? No, he no longer hates Ida. He does quite like to watch Westerns; maybe he will see her up on the screen one day. Perhaps, he says to himself, perhaps he actually should try visiting Hamsun again.

46.

Poor Ida. She trudges from one audition to the next. No more films materialize for her. A theater on Hollywood Boulevard does offer her a booking as an understudy, but when she dyes her platinum-blonde hair brown for the role, she suddenly has several sudsy clumps in her hand, she looks awful, and then she is simply let go once more, four dollars' compensation in her pocket, out to palm-lined Gower; good grief, they tell her, she really ought to count her blessings.

Chaplin does not answer the telephone, or no one puts her through; every day she rings him up multiple times, but it is no use, after all he has so unbelievably many appointments, she tells herself, or else he does not remember (how could that be after he so very obviously recognized her some weeks ago?), maybe this is just how America is: full of broken promises and wanton disappointments.

Presently she is given notice to vacate her room, the electricity has already been shut off, she muddles through week by week. For days on end she slinks around the pawnshop with her clip-on earrings in hand. At least at the diner on Cahuenga she can still put fried eggs and bacon on her tab; they like her there.

One afternoon, a Brazilian gentleman (pencil mustache, cigarillo, enameled Art Deco ring on his pinky finger) addresses her at the diner as she sits in front of her twelfth cup of free coffee. He takes her along with him to his villa in the canyons; already waiting there in the recessed, velvet-cushioned living room are other thin young girls. They are offered brandy and heroin; she declines but has to think about it at length.

The Brazilian arranges the girls on the pillows; some of them strip naked; one or two film cameras are running; an assistant brings a large wooden baseball bat from the kitchen; the door to the house is bolted from the inside. Ida panics and is slapped in the face. Outside the sprinklers are twirling and spraying billions of the finest drops, which coalesce wondrously to form a rainbow, only then to drip down again off the foliage and succulents into the sparse, beflowered Californian shrubbery.

Ida screams and screams. The assistant opens a glass sliding door for her, she stumbles out barefoot onto the lawn, hastens through the shimmer of falling drops of water from the sprinkler system, her short, beige, filigree silk gown becomes wet and transparent, and one of the cameramen trailing behind films her faltering, whimpering, running away—mocking laughter follows her out of the villa.

Back outside her apartment building she finds the lock to her door changed and her belongings and furniture placed out in front and on the sidewalk. A few passersby have already helped themselves to her things and walked off with this or that. She sits down on the curb, hugging her knees, and considers whether she ought to cry.

Above her, up in the bone-dry hills, she glimpses the gigantic *menetekel* of the *Hollywoodland* sign beneath the immaculate blue of the sky. Masahiko appears to her, the man who truly touched her body for the first time. But perhaps she also misses Nägeli. That this was bound to happen, fine, that wasn't really the plan. Actually, there was never any plan at all.

It is already evening when she ascends the framework

of the *H*. Beneath and before her, clearly recognizable through the metal struts, lies shimmering and blazing the boundless city whose infinite expanse seems to join up at the ultramarine horizon with the gradually blackening night sky; up to that point there is an enigmatic, elastic flatness, which the simple grid of intersecting boulevards, welling up in golden yellow from the car headlights, extends through perspective into the distance.

Higher and higher Ida climbs, sitting astride the steel-framed edge of the letter, now bringing the other leg over to the front. Oh, now that's odd, she thinks: an *H*, exactly like in my dream. There is a forgetting of all existence, a silencing of our being where we feel as if we have found everything.

Her head sinks down until the vertex of her secure grip is exceeded, she slips off, tries to grab hold at the last moment, calls out in astonishment, falls noisily and far, and her plunging, tumbling body eventually comes to rest, draped over cacti whose sharp, merciless spines have lacerated, yes, almost flayed the skin from her face.

They come with an ambulance and a hearse, parking all the way up on Mulholland. A gaunt coyote, lured by the smell of blood, quietly slinks back into the bushes. Three policemen take notes by the light of the flood lamps; one has bashfully turned aside to vomit. Down

below, at the exit to the canyon, the lights of Los Angeles eternally hiss their encoded messages.

Ida's half-naked body is carefully laid onto a stretcher,
but before she is lifted into the hearse, a journalist will
flash a few pictures of her disturbingly lacerated face,
which he will later sell to a magazine specializing in
spectacular fatalities. In these writings it will read that
she was like a fire sleeping in flint.

A Note About the Author

Christian Kracht is a Swiss novelist whose books have been translated into thirty languages. His latest novel, *The Dead*, was the recipient of the Hermann Hesse Literature Prize and the Swiss Book Prize.

A Note About the Translator

Daniel Bowles teaches German studies at Boston College. For his translation of Christian Kracht's *Imperium* he was awarded the 2016 Helen and Kurt Wolff Translator's Prize. He has also translated novels by Thomas Meinecke and works by Alexander Kluge, Rainald Goetz, and Xaver Bayer.